The Hamilton family of
Greyoaks, South Carolina
cordially invites you to the wedding of

Blake Hamilton

and

Kathryn Mary Kilpatrick

on the morning of September 12th

Please address questions and book requests to: Silhouette Reader Service
U.S.: 3010 Walden Ave., P.O. Box 1325, Buffalo, NY 14269
Canadian: P.O. Box 609, Fort Erie, Ont. L2A 5X3

Western Weddings

DIANA PALMER

SEPTEMBER MORNING

Silhouette Books

Published by Silhouette Books
America's Publisher of Contemporary Romance

SILHOUETTE BOOKS
300 East 42nd St.,
New York, N.Y. 10017

ISBN 0-373-30112-X

SEPTEMBER MORNING

Copyright © 1982 by Diana Palmer

Celebrity Wedding Certificates published by permission of Donald Ray Pounders from *Celebrity Wedding Ceremonies*.

Printed in U.S.A.

A Letter from the Author

Dear Reader,

South Carolina is one of the most beautiful states I've ever visited, and it's located very close to my home in Northeast Georgia. I fell in love with it years ago and it was my pleasure to set my first Silhouette Desire, *September Morning*, there.

I've spent many a happy hour driving around that fascinating state and visiting historical locations there. I hope my delight in South Carolina comes through on the pages of this book. It was fun to write. I hope it's fun to read, too.

All my best,

Diana Palmer

To Ann, Anne, "George,"
"Eddard," Dannis and Dad

One

The meadow was dew-misted, and the morning had the nip of a September breeze to give it life. Kathryn Mary Kilpatrick tossed her long black hair and laughed with the sheer joy of being alive. The sound startled the chestnut gelding she was riding, making it dance nervously over the damp ground.

"Easy, boy," she said soothingly, her gloved hand reaching out to touch his mane gently.

He calmed, reacting to the familiar caress. Sundance had been hers since he was a colt, a present from Blake on her sixteenth birthday. Sundance was a mature five-year-old now, but some of his coltish uncertainties lingered. He was easily startled and high-strung. Like Kathryn Mary.

Her dark green eyes shimmered with excitement as she studied the long horizon under the pink and amber swirls of the dawn sky. It was so good to be home again. The exclusive girls' school had polished her manners and given her the poise of a model, but it had done nothing to cool her ardor for life or to dampen the passion she felt for Greyoaks. Despite the fact that the Hamiltons' South Carolina farm was her home by adoption, not by birth, she loved every green, rolling hill and pine forest of it, just as though she were a Hamilton herself.

A flash of color caught her attention, and she wheeled Sundance as Phillip Hamilton came tearing across the meadow toward her on a thoroughbred Arabian with a coat like polished black leather. She smiled, watching him. If Blake ever caught him riding one of his prize breeding stallions like that, it would mean disaster. What luck for Phillip that Blake was in Europe on business. Maude might indulge her youngest, but Blake indulged no one.

"Hi!" Phillip called breathlessly. He reined in just in front of her and caught his wind, tossing back his unruly brown hair with a restless hand. His brown eyes twinkled with mischief as they swept over her slender figure in the chic riding habit. But the mischief went out of them when he noticed her bare head.

"No helmet?" he chided.

She pouted at him with her full, soft lips. "Don't scold," she accused. "It was just a little ride, and I hate wearing a hard hat all the time."

"One fall and you'd be done for," he observed.

"You sound just like Blake!"

He smiled at her mutinous look. "Too bad he missed your homecoming. Oh, well, he'll be back at the end of the week—just in time for the Barringtons' party."

"Blake hates parties," she reminded him. Her eyes lowered to the rich leather of her Western saddle. "And he hates me too, most of the time."

"He doesn't," Phillip returned. "It's just that you set fire to his temper, you rebellious little witch. I can remember a time when you all but worshiped my big brother."

She grimaced, turning her eyes to the long horizon where thoroughbred Arabians grazed on lush pasture grass, their black coats shimmering like oil in the sunlight. "Did I?" She laughed shortly. "He was kind to me once, when my mother died."

"He cares about you. We all do," he said gently.

She smiled at him warmly and reached out an impulsive hand to touch his sleeve. "I'm ungrateful, and I don't mean to be. You and your mother have been wonderful to me. Taking me in, putting me through school—how could I be ungrateful?"

"Blake had a little to do with it," he reminded her wryly.

She tossed her hair back impatiently. "I suppose," she admitted grudgingly.

"Finishing school was his idea."

"And I hated it!" she flashed. "I wanted to go to the university and take political science courses."

"Blake likes to entertain buyers," he reminded her. "Political science courses don't teach you how to be a hostess."

She shrugged. "Well, I'm not going to be here forever, despite the fact that you and Blake are my cousins," she said. "I'll get married someday. I know I owe your family a lot, but I'm not going to spend my whole life playing hostess for Blake! He can get married and let his wife do it. If he can find anyone brave enough," she added waspishly.

"You've got to be kidding, Cuz," he chuckled. "They follow him around like ants on a sugar trail. Blake could have his pick when it comes to women, and you know it."

"It must be his money, then," she said tightly, "because it sure isn't his cheerful personality that draws them!"

"You're just sore because he wouldn't let you go away with Jack Harris for the weekend," he teased.

She flushed right up to her hairline. "I didn't know Jack had planned for us to be alone at the cottage," she protested. "I thought his parents were going to be there, too."

"But you didn't think to check. Blake did." He laughed at her expression. "I'll never forget how he looked when Jack came to get you. Or how Jack looked when he left, alone."

She shivered at the memory. "I'd like to forget."

"I'll bet you would. You've been staring daggers at Blake ever since, but it just bounces right off. You don't dent him, do you?"

"Nothing dents Blake," she murmured. "He just stands there and lets me rant and rave until he's had enough, then he turns that cold voice on me and walks away. He'll be glad when I'm gone," she said in a quiet voice.

"You're not going anywhere yet, are you?" he asked suddenly.

She darted a mischievous glance at him. "I *had* thought about joining the French Foreign Legion," she admitted. "Do you think I could get my application accepted before the weekend?"

He laughed. "In time to escape Blake? You know you've missed him."

"I have?" she asked with mock innocence.

"Six months is a long time. He's calmed down."

"Blake never forgets," she sighed miserably. She stared past Phillip to the towering gray stone house in the distance with its graceful arches and the cluster of huge live oaks dripping Spanish moss that stood like sentries around it.

"Don't work yourself into a nervous breakdown," Phillip said comfortingly. "Come on, race me back to the house and we'll have breakfast."

She sighed wearily. "All right."

Maude's dark eyes lit up when the two of them walked into the elegant dining room and seated themselves at the polished oak table.

She had the same olive skin and sharp, dark eyes as her eldest son, the same forthright manner and quick temper. Maude was nothing like Phillip. She lacked his gentleness and easy manner, as well as his pale coloring. Those traits came from his late father, not from his maverick mother, who thought nothing of getting a congressman out of bed at two in the morning if she wanted a piece of pending legislation explained to her.

"It's good to have you home, baby," Maude told Kathryn, reaching out a slender, graceful hand to touch the younger woman's arm. "I'm simply surrounded by men these days."

"That's the truth," Phillip said wryly as he helped himself to scrambled eggs from the bone china platter. "Matt Davis and Jack Nelson nearly came to blows over her at a cocktail party last week."

Maude glared at him. "That isn't so," she protested.

"Oh?" Kathryn asked with an impish smile as she sipped her black coffee.

Maude shifted uncomfortably. "Anyway, I wish Blake were home. It was bad timing, that crisis at the London office. I had a special evening planned for Friday night. A homecoming party for you. It would have been perfect . . ."

"I don't need Blake to make a party perfect," Kathryn burst out without thinking.

Maude's pencil-thin gray brows went up. "Are you going to hold it against him forever?" she chided.

Kathryn's fingers tightened around her coffee cup. "He didn't have to be so rough on me!" she protested.

"He was right, Kathryn Mary, and you know it," Maude said levelly. She leaned forward, resting her forearms on the table. "Darling, you have to remember that you're just barely twenty. Blake's thirty-four now, and he knows a great deal more about life than you've had time to learn. We've all sheltered you," she added, frowning. "Sometimes I wonder if it was quite fair."

"Ask Blake," she returned bitterly. "He's kept me under glass for years."

"His protective instinct," Phillip said with an amused grin. "A misplaced mother hen complex."

"I wouldn't let him hear that, if I were you," Maude commented drily.

"I'm not afraid of big brother," he replied. "Just because he can outfight me is no reason...on second thought, you may have a point."

Maude laughed. "You're a delight. I wish Blake had a little of your ability to take things lightly. He's so intense."

"I can think of a better word," Kathryn said under her breath.

"Isn't it amazing," Phillip asked his mother, "how brave she is when Blake isn't here?"

"Amazing." Maude nodded. She smiled at Kathryn. "Cheer up, sweetheart. Let me tell you what Eve Barrington has planned for your homecoming party Saturday night...the one I was going to give you if Blake hadn't been called away..."

* * *

The arrangements for the party were faultless, Kathryn discovered. The florist had delivered urns of dried flowers in blazing fall colors, and tasteful arrangements of daisies and mums and baby's breath to decorate the buffet tables. The intimate little gathering at the nearby estate swelled to over fifty people, not all of them contemporaries of Kathryn's. Quite a number, she noticed with amusement, were politicians. Maude was lobbying fiercely for legislation to protect a nearby stretch of South Carolina's unspoiled river land from being zoned for business. No doubt she'd pleaded with Eve to add those politicians to the guest list, Kathryn thought wickedly.

Nan Barrington, Eve's daughter, and one of Kathryn's oldest friends, pulled her aside while the musicians launched into a frantic rock number.

"Mother hates hard rock," she confided as the band blared out. "I can't imagine why she hired that particular band, when it's all they play."

"The name," Kathryn guessed. "It's the Glen Miller ensemble, and Glen spells his name with just one 'n.' Your mother probably thought they played the same kind of music as the late Glenn Miller."

"That's Mother," Nan agreed with a laugh. She ran a finger over the rim of her glass, filled with sparkling rum punch. Her blond hair sparkled with the same amber color as she looked around the room. "I thought Blake was going to come by when he got home. It's after ten now."

Kathryn smiled at her indulgently. Nan had had a crush on Blake since their early teens. Blake pretended not to notice, treating both girls like the adolescents he thought them.

"You know Blake hates parties," she reminded the shorter girl.

"It can't be for lack of partners to take to them," Nan sighed.

Kathryn frowned at her. She cupped her own glass in her hands and wondered why that statement nagged her. She knew Blake dated, but it had been a long time since she'd spent more than a few days at Greyoaks. Not for years. There was too much to do. Relatives she could visit in faraway places like France and Greece and even Australia. Cruises with friends like Nan. School events and girlfriends to visit and parties to go to. There hadn't been much reason to stay at Greyoaks. Especially since that last bout with Blake over Jack Harris. She sighed, remembering how harsh he'd been about it. Jack Harris had turned every color in the rainbow before Blake got through telling him what he thought in that cold, precise voice that always accompanied his temper.

When he'd turned it on Kathryn, it had been all she could manage not to run. She was honestly afraid of Blake. Not that he'd beat her or anything. It was a different kind of fear, strange and ever-present, growing as she matured.

"Why the frown?" Nan asked suddenly.

"Was I frowning?" She laughed. She shrugged, sipping her punch. Her eyes ran over her shorter friend's pale blue evening gown, held up by tiny spaghetti straps. "I love your dress."

"It isn't a patch on yours," Nan sighed, wistfully eyeing the Grecian off-the-shoulder style of Kathryn's delicate white gown. The wisps of chiffon foamed and floated with every movement. "It's a dream."

"I have a friend in Atlanta who's a budding designer," she explained with a smile. "This is from her first collection. She had a showing at that new department store on Peachtree Street."

"Everything looks good on you," Nan said genuinely. "You're so tall and willowy."

"Skinny, Blake says." She laughed and then suddenly froze as she looked across the room straight into a pair of narrow, dark eyes in a face as hard as granite.

He was as tall and big as she remembered, all hard-muscled grace and blatant masculinity. His head was bare, his dark hair gleaming in the light from the crystal chandelier overhead. His deeply tanned face had its own inborn arrogance, a legacy from his grandfather, who had forged a small empire from the ashes of the old confederacy. His eyes were cold, even at a distance, his mouth chiseled and firm and just a little cruel. Kathryn shivered involuntarily as his eyes trailed up and down the revealing dress she was wearing, clearly disapproving.

Nan followed her gaze, and her small face lit up. "It's Blake!" she exclaimed. "Kathryn, aren't you going to say hello to him?"

She swallowed. "Oh, yes, of course," she said, aware of Maude going forward to greet her eldest and Phillip waving to him carelessly from across the room.

"You don't look terribly enthusiastic about it," Nan remarked, studying the flush in her friend's cheeks and the slight tremor in the slender hands that held the crystal glass.

"He'll be furious because I haven't got a bow in my hair and a teddy bear under my arm," she said with a mirthless laugh.

"You're not a little girl anymore," Nan said, coming to her friend's defense despite her attraction to Blake.

"Tell Blake," she sighed. "See?" she murmured as he lifted his arrogant head and motioned for her to join him. "I'm being summoned."

"Could you manage to look a little less like Marie Antoinette on her way to the guillotine?" Nan whispered.

"I can't help it. My neck's tingling. See you," she muttered, moving toward Blake with a faint smile.

She moved forward, through the throng of guests, her heart throbbing as heavily as the rock rhythm that shook the walls around her. Six months hadn't erased the bitterness of their last quarrel, and judging by the look on Blake's rugged face, it was still fresh in his mind, too.

He drew deeply on his cigarette, looking down his straight nose at her, and she couldn't help noticing how dangerously attractive he was in his dark evening clothes. The white silk of his shirt was a perfect foil for his olive complexion, his arrogant good looks. The tang of his Oriental cologne drifted down into her nostrils, a fragrance that echoed his vibrant masculinity.

"Hello, Blake," she said nervously, glad Maude had vanished into the throng of politicians so she didn't have to pretend more enthusiasm.

His eyes sketched her slender figure, lingering at the plunging neckline that revealed tantalizing glimpses of the swell of her small, high breasts.

"Advertising, Kate?" he asked harshly. "I thought you'd learned your lesson with Harris."

"Don't call me Kate," she fired back. "And it's no more revealing than what everyone else is wearing."

"You haven't changed," he sighed indulgently. "All fire and lace and wobbly legs. I hoped that finishing school might give you a little maturity."

Her emerald eyes burned. "I'm twenty, Blake!"

One dark eyebrow went up. "What do you want me to do about it?"

She started to reply that she didn't want him to do a thing, but the anger faded away suddenly. "Oh, Blake," she moaned, "why do you have to spoil my party? It's been such fun..."

"For whom?" he asked, his eyes finding several of the politicians present. "You or Maude?"

"She's trying to save the wildlife along the Edisto River," she said absently. "They want to develop part of the riverfront."

"Yes, let's save the water moccasins and sand-flies, at all costs!" he agreed lightly, although Kathryn knew he was as avid a conservationist as Maude.

She peeked up at him. "I seem to remember that you went on television to support that wilderness proposal on the national forest."

He raised his cigarette to his firm lips. "Guilty," he admitted with a faint, rare smile. He glanced toward the band and the smile faded. "Are they all playing the same song?" he asked irritably.

"I'm not sure. I thought you liked music," she teased.

He glowered down at her. "I do. But that," he added with a speaking glance in the band's direction, "isn't."

"My generation thinks it is," she replied with a challenge in her bright eyes. "And if you don't like contemporary music, then why did you bother to come to the party, you old stick-in-the-mud?"

He reached down and tapped her on the cheek with a long, stinging finger. "Don't be smart," he told her. "I came because I hadn't seen you for six months, if you want the truth."

"Why? So you could drive me home and bawl me out in privacy on the way?" she asked.

His heavy dark brows came together. "How much of that punch have you had?" he asked curtly.

"Not quite enough," she replied with an impudent grin and tossed off the rest of the punch in her glass.

"Feeling reckless, little girl?" he asked quietly.

"It's more like self-preservation, Blake," she admitted softly, peeking up at him over the empty glass as she held its coolness to her pink lips. "I was getting my nerves numb so that it wouldn't bother me when you started giving me hell."

He took a draw from his cigarette. "It was six months ago," he said tightly. "I've forgotten it."

"No you haven't," she sighed, reading the cold anger very near the surface in his taut face. "I really didn't know what Jack had in mind. I probably should have, but I'm not very worldly."

He sighed heavily. "No, that's for sure. I used to think it was a good thing. But the older you get, the more I wonder."

"That's just what Maude was saying," she murmured, wondering if he could read people's minds.

"And she could be right." His eyes narrowed to a glittering darkness as he studied her in the revealing little dress. "That dress is years too old for you."

"Does that mean it's all right with you if I grow up?" she asked sweetly.

One dark eyebrow rose laconically. "I wasn't aware that you needed my permission."

"I seem to, though," she persisted. "If I try to do anything about it, you'll be on my neck like a duck after a June bug."

"That depends on what sort of growing-up process you have in mind," he replied, reaching over to crush the cigarette into an ashtray. "Promiscuity is definitely out."

"Not in your case, it isn't!"

His head jerked up, his eyes blazing. "What the hell has my private life got to do with you?" he asked in a voice that cut like sheer ice.

She felt like backing away. "I . . . I was just teasing, Blake," she defended in a shaken whisper.

"I'm not laughing," he said curtly.

"You never do with me," she said in a voice like china breaking.

"Stop acting like a silly adolescent."

She bit her lower lip, trying to stem the welling tears in her soft, hurt eyes. "If you'll excuse me," she said unsteadily, "I'll go back and play with my dolls. Thank you for your warm welcome," she added in a tiny voice before she pushed her way through the crowd away from him. For the first time, she wished she'd never come to live with Blake's family.

Two

For the rest of the evening she avoided Blake, sticking to Nan and Phillip like a shadow while she nursed her emotional wounds. Not that Blake seemed to notice. He was standing with Maude and one of the younger congressmen in the group, deep in discussion.

"I wonder what they're talking about now?" Phillip asked as he danced Kathryn around the room to one of the band's few slow tunes.

"Saving water moccasins," she muttered, her full lips pouting, her eyes as dark as jade with hurt.

Phillip sighed heavily. "What's he done now?"

"What?" she asked, lifting her flushed face to Phillip's patiently amused eyes.

"Blake. He hasn't been in the same room with you for ten minutes, and the two of you are already avoiding one another. Talk about repeat acts!"

Her rounded jaw clenched. "He hates me, I told you he did."

"What's he done?" he repeated.

She glared at his top shirt button. "He said . . . he said I couldn't be promiscuous."

"Good for Blake," Phillip said with annoying enthusiasm.

"You don't understand. That was just what started it," she explained. "And I was teasing him about not being a monk, and he jumped all over me about digging into his private life." She felt herself tense as she remembered the blazing heat of Blake's anger. "I didn't mean anything."

"You didn't know about Della?" he asked softly.

She gaped up at him. "Della who?"

"Della Ness. He just broke it off with her," he explained.

A pang of something shivered through her slender body, and she wondered why the thought of Blake with a woman should cause a sensation like that. "Were they engaged?"

He laughed softly. "No."

She blushed. "Oh."

"She's been bothering him ever since, calling up and crying and sending him letters...you know how that would affect him." He whirled her around in time to the music and brought her back against him loosely. "It hasn't helped his temper any. I think he was glad for the European trip. She hasn't called in over a week."

"Maybe he's missing her," she said.

"Blake? Miss a woman? Honey, you know better than that. Blake is the original self-sufficient male. He never gets emotionally involved with his women."

She toyed with the lapel of his evening jacket. "He doesn't have to take his irritation out on me," she protested sullenly. "And at my homecoming party, too."

"Jet lag," Phillip told her. He stopped as the music did and grimaced when the hard rock blared out again. "Let's sit this one out," he yelled above it. "My legs get tangled trying to dance to that."

He drew her off the floor and back to the open veranda, leading her onto the plant-studded balcony with a friendly hand clasping hers.

"Don't let Blake spoil this for you," he said gently as they stood leaning on the stone balustrade, looking out over the city lights of King's Fort that twinkled jewel-bright on the dark horizon. "He's had a hard week. That strike at the London mill wasn't easily settled.''

She nodded, remembering that one of the corporation's biggest textile mills was located there, and that this was nowhere near the first strike that had halted production.

''It's been nothing but trouble,'' Phillip added with a hard sigh. ''I don't see why Blake doesn't close it down. We've enough mills in New York and Alabama to more than take up the slack.''

Her fingers toyed with the cool leaves of an elephant-ear plant near the balcony's edge as she listened to Phillip's pleasant voice. He was telling her how much more solvent the corporation would be if they bought two more yarn mills to add to the conglomerate, and how many spindles each one would need to operate, and how new equipment could increase production . . . and all she was hearing was Blake's deep, angry voice.

It wasn't her fault that his discarded mistresses couldn't take ''no'' for an answer, and it was hardly prying into his private life to state that he had women. Her face reddened, just thinking of Blake with a woman in his big arms, his massive torso bare and bronzed, a woman's soft body crushed against the hair-covered chest where muscles rippled and surged . . .

The blush got worse. She was shocked by her own thoughts. She'd only seen Blake stripped to the waist once or twice, but the sight had stayed with her. He was all muscle, and that wedge of black, curling hair that laced down to his belt buckle somehow emphasized his blatant maleness. It wasn't hard to understand the effect he had on women. Kathryn tried not to think about it. She'd always been able to separate the Blake who was like family from the arrogant, attractive Blake who drew women like flies everywhere he went. She'd kept her eyes on his dark face and reminded herself that he had watched her grow from adolescence to womanhood and he knew too much about her to find her attractive in any adult way. He knew that she threw things when she lost her temper, that she never refilled the water trays when she emptied the ice out of them. He knew that she took off her shoes in church, and climbed trees to hide from the minister when he came visiting on Sunday afternoon. He even knew that she sometimes threw her worn blouses behind the door instead of in the clothes hamper. She sighed heavily. He knew too much, all right.

"...Kathryn!"

She jumped. "Sorry, Phil," she said quickly, "I was drinking in the night. What did you say?"

He shook his head, laughing. "Never mind, darling, it wasn't important. Feeling better now?"

"I wasn't drunk," she said accusingly.

"Just a little tipsy, though," he grinned. "Three glasses of punch, wasn't it? And mother emptied the liquor cabinet into it with our hostess's smiling approval."

"I didn't realize how strong it was," Kathryn admitted.

"It has a cumulative effect. Want to go back in?"

"Must we?" she asked. "Couldn't we slip out the side door and go see that new sci-fi movie downtown?"

"Run out on your own party? Shame on you!"

"I'm ashamed," she agreed. "Can we?"

"Can we *what?*"

"Go see the movie. Oh, come on, Phil," she pleaded, "save me from him. I'll lie for you. I'll tell Maude I kidnapped you at gunpoint..."

"Will you, now?" Maude laughed, coming up behind them. "Why do you want to kidnap Phillip?"

"There's a new science fiction movie in town, and..." Kathryn began.

"... and it would keep you out of Blake's way until morning, is that how this song goes?" Phillip's mother guessed keenly.

Kathryn sighed, clasping her hands in front of her. "That's the chorus," she admitted.

"Never mind, he's gone."

She looked up quickly. "Blake?"

"Blake." Maude laughed softly. "Cursing the band, the punch, the politicians, jet lag, labor unions, smog and women with a noticeable lack of tact until Eve almost wept with relief when he announced that he was going home to bed."

"I hope the slats fall out under him," Kathryn said pleasantly.

"They're box springs," Maude commented absently. "I bought it for him last year for his birthday, remember, when he complained that he couldn't get any rest..."

"I hope the box springs collapse, then," Kathryn corrected.

"Malicious little thing, aren't you?" Phillip asked teasingly.

Maude slumped wearily. "Not again. Really, Kathryn Mary, this never-ending war between you and my eldest is going to give me ulcers! What's he done this time?"

"He told her she couldn't be promiscuous," Phillip obliged, "and got mad at her when she pointed out that he believed in the double standard."

"Kathryn! You didn't say that to Blake!"

Kathryn looked vaguely embarrassed. "I was just teasing."

"Oh, my darling, you're so lucky you weren't near any bodies of water that he could have pitched you into," Maude said. "He's been absolutely black-tempered ever since that Della toy of his started getting possessive and he sent her packing. You remember, Phil, it was about the time Kathryn wrote that she was going to Crete on that cruise with Missy Donavan and her brother Lawrence."

"Speaking of Lawrence," Phillip said, drawling out the name dramatically, "what happened?"

"He's coming to see me when he flies down for that writers' convention on the coast," she said with a smile. "He just sold another mystery novel and he's wild with enthusiasm."

"Is he planning to spend a few days?" Maude asked. "Blake has been suspicious of writers, you know, ever since that reporter did a story about his affair with the beauty contest girl...who was she again, Phil?"

"Larry isn't a reporter," Kathryn argued, "he only writes fiction..."

"That's exactly what that story about Blake and the beauty was," Phillip grinned. "Fiction."

"Will you listen?" Maude grumbled. "You simply can't invite Lawrence into the house while Blake's home. I've got the distinct impression he's already prejudiced against the man.''

"Larry isn't a pushover," Kathryn replied, remembering her friend's hot temper and red hair.

Maude frowned, thinking. "Phillip, maybe you could call that Della person and give her Blake's unlisted number just before Kathryn Mary's friend comes, and I'll remind him of how lovely St. Martin is in the summer..."

"It will only be for two or three days," Kathryn protested. Her soft young features tightened. "I thought Greyoaks was my home, too..."

Maude's thin face cleared instantly and she drew Kathryn into her arms. "Oh, darling, of course it is, you know it is! It's just that it's Blake's home as well, and that's the problem."

"Just because Larry's a writer..."

"That isn't the only reason," Maude sighed, patting her back. "Blake's very possessive of you, Kathryn. He doesn't like you dating older men, especially men like Jack Harris."

"He has to let go someday," Kathryn said stubbornly, drawing away from Maude. "I'm a woman now, not the adolescent he used to buy bubble gum for. I have a right to my own friends."

"You're asking for trouble if you start a rebellion with Blake in his present mood," Maude cautioned.

Kathryn lifted a hand to touch her dark hair as the breeze blew a tiny wisp of it into the corner of her mouth. "Just don't tell him Larry's coming," she said, raising her face defiantly.

Phillip stared at Maude. "Is her insurance paid up?" he asked conversationally.

"Blake controls the checkbook for all of us," Maude reminded her. "You could find yourself without an allowance at all; even without your car."

"No revolution succeeds without sacrifice," Kathryn said proudly.

"Oh, good grief," Phillip said, turning away.

"Come back here," Kathryn called after him. "I'm not through!"

Maude burst out laughing. "I think he's going to light a candle for you. If you're planning to take Blake on, you may need a prayer or two."

"Or Blake may," Kathryn shot back.

Maude only laughed.

The house was quiet when they got home, and Maude let out a sigh of pure relief.

"So far, so good," she said smiling at Kathryn and Phillip. "Now, if we can just sneak up the stairs..."

"Why are you sneaking around at all?" came a deep, irritated voice from the general direction of the study.

Kathryn felt all her new resolutions deserting her as she whirled and found herself staring straight into Blake's dark, angry eyes.

She dropped her gaze, and her heart thumped wildly in her chest as she dimly heard Maude explaining why the three of them were being so quiet.

"We knew you'd be tired, dear," Maude told him gently.

"Tired, my foot," he returned, lifting a glass of amber liquid in a shot glass to his hard, chiseled mouth. He glared at Kathryn over its rim. "You knew I'd had it out with Kate."

"She's been gorging herself on the rum punch, Blake," Phillip said with a grin. "Announcing her independence and preparing for holy revolution."

"Oh, please, shut up," Kathryn managed in a tortured whisper.

"But, darling, you were so brave at the Barringtons," Phillip chided. "Don't you want to martyr yourself to the cause of freedom?"

"No, I want to be sick," she corrected, swallowing hard. She glanced up at Blake's hard-set face. The harsh words all came back, and she wished fervently that she'd accepted Nan's invitation to spend the night.

Blake swirled the amber liquid in his glass absently. "Good night, Mother, Phil."

Maude threw Kathryn an apologetic glance as she headed for the staircase with Phillip right behind.

"You wouldn't rather discuss the merger with the Banes Corporation?" Phillip grinned at Blake. "It would be a lot quieter."

"Oh, don't desert me," Kathryn called after them.

"You declared war, darling," Phillip called back, "and I believe in a strict policy of non-interference."

She locked her hands behind her, shivering in her warm sable coat despite the warmth of the house and the hot darkness of Blake's eyes.

"Well, go ahead," she muttered, dropping her gaze to the open neck of his white silk shirt. 'You've already taken one bite out of me, you might as well have an arm or two."

He chuckled softly and, surprised, she jerked her face up to find amusement in his eyes.

"Come in here and talk to me," he said, turning to lead the way back into his walnut-paneled study. His big Irish Setter, Hunter, rose and wagged his tail, and Blake ruffled his fur affectionately as he settled down in the wing armchair in front of the fireplace.

Kathryn took the chair across from his, absently darting a glance at the wood decoratively piled up in the hearth. "Daddy used to burn it," she remarked, using the affectionate name she gave Blake's father, even though he was barely a distant cousin. He was like the father she'd lost.

"So do I, when I need to take the chill off. But it isn't cool enough tonight," he replied.

She studied his big, husky body and wondered if he ever felt the cold. Warmth seemed to radiate from him at close range, as if fires burned under that darkly tanned skin.

He tossed off the rest of his drink and linked his hands behind his head. His dark eyes pinned Kathryn to her chair. "Why don't you get out of that coat and stop trying to look as if you're ten minutes late for an appointment somewhere?"

"I'm cold, Blake," she murmured.

"Turn up the thermostat, then."

"I won't be here that long, will I?" she asked hopefully.

His dark, quiet eyes traveled over the soft, pink skin revealed by her white dress, making her feel very young and uncomfortable.

"Must you stare at me like that?" she asked uneasily. She toyed with a wisp of chiffon.

He pulled his cigarette case from his pocket and took his time about lighting up. "What's this about a revolution?" he asked conversationally.

She blinked at him. "Oh, what Phil said?" she asked, belatedly comprehending. She swallowed hard. "Uh, I just..."

He laughed shortly. "Kathryn, I can't remember a conversation with you that didn't end in stammers."

Her full lips pouted. "I wouldn't stammer if you wouldn't jump on me every time you get the chance."

One heavy dark eyebrow went up. He looked completely relaxed, imperturbable. That composure rattled her, and she couldn't help wondering if anything ever made him lose it.

"Do I?" he asked.

"You know very well you do." She studied the hard lines of his face, noting the faint tautness of fatigue that only a stranger would miss. "You're very tired, aren't you?" she asked suddenly, warming to him.

He took a draw from the cigarette. "Dead," he admitted.

"Then why aren't you in bed?" she wanted to know.

He studied her quietly. "I didn't mean to ruin the party for you."

The old, familiar tenderness in his voice brought an annoying mist to her eyes and she averted them. "It's all right."

"No, it isn't." He flicked ashes into the receptacle beside his chair, and a huge sigh lifted his chest. "Kate, I just broke off an affair. The silly woman's pestering me to death, and when you said what you did, I overreacted." He shrugged. "My temper's a little on edge lately, or I'd have laughed it off."

She smiled at him faintly. "Did you...love her?" she asked gently.

He burst out laughing. "What a child you are," he chuckled. "Do I have to love a woman to take her into my bed?"

The flush went all the way down her throat. "I don't know," she admitted.

"No," he said, the smile fading, "I don't suppose you do. I believed in love, at your age."

"Cynic," she accused.

He crushed out the cigarette in his ashtray. "Guilty. I've learned that sex is better without emotional blinders."

She dropped her eyes in mortification, trying not to see the unholy amusement on his dark face.

"Embarrassed, Kate?" he chided. "I thought that experience with Harris had matured you."

Her green eyes flashed fire as they lifted to meet his. "Do we have to go through this again?" she asked.

"Not if you've learned something from it." His gaze dropped pointedly to her dress. "Although I have my doubts. Are you wearing anything under that damned nightgown?"

"Blake!" she burst out. "It's not a nightgown!"

"It looks like one."

"It's the style!"

He stared her down. "In Paris, I hear, the style is a vest with nothing under it, worn open."

She tossed her hair angrily. "And if I lived in Paris, I'd wear one," she threw back.

He only smiled. "Would you?" His eyes dropped again to her bodice, and the boldness of his gaze made her feel strange sensations. "I wonder."

She clasped her hands in her lap, feeling outwitted and outmatched. "What did you want to talk to me about, Blake?" she asked.

"I've invited some people over for a visit."

She remembered her own invitation to Lawrence Donavan, and she held her breath. "Uh, who?" she asked politely.

"Dick Leeds and his daughter Vivian," he told her. "They're going to be here for a week or so while

Dick and I iron out that labor mess. He's the head of the local union, that's giving us so much trouble.''

"And his daughter?'' she asked, hating herself for her own curiosity.

"Blond and sexy,'' he mused.

She glared at him. "Just your style,'' she shot at him. "With the emphasis on sexy.''

He watched her with silent amusement. Blake, the adult, indulging his ward. She wanted to throw something at him.

"Well, I hope you don't expect me to help Maude keep them entertained,'' she said. "Because I'm expecting some company of my own!''

The danger signals were flashing out of his deep brown eyes. "What company?'' he asked curtly.

She lifted her chin bravely. "Lawrence Donavan.''

Something took fire and exploded under his jutting brow.

"Not in my house,'' he said in a tone that might have cut diamond.

"But, Blake, I've already invited him!'' she wailed.

"You heard me. If you didn't want to be embarrassed, you should have consulted with me before inviting him,'' he added roughly. "What were you going to do, Kathryn, meet him at the airport and then tell me about it? A *fait accompli?*"

She couldn't meet his eyes. "Something like that."

"Cable him. Tell him something came up."

She lifted her eyes and glared at him, sitting there like a conqueror, ordering her life. If she buckled under one more time, she'd never be able to stand up to him. Never. She couldn't let him win this time.

Her jaw set stubbornly. "No."

He got to his feet slowly, gracefully for such a big man, and the set of his broad shoulders was intimidating even without the sudden, fierce narrowing of his eyes.

"What did you say?" he asked in a deceptively soft tone.

She laced her fingers together in front of her and clenched them. "I said no," she managed in a rasping voice. Her dark green eyes appealed to him. "Blake, it's my home, too. At least, you said it was the day you asked me to come live here," she reminded him.

"I didn't say you could use it as a rendezvous for romantic trysts!"

"You bring women here," she tossed back, remembering with a surge of anguish the night when she had accidentally come home too early from a date and found him with Jessica King on the very chairs where they were now sitting. Jessica had been stripped to the waist, and so had Blake. Kathryn had barely even noticed the blonde, her eyes were so staggered by the sight of Blake with his broad, muscled chest bared by the woman's exploring hands. She'd never been able to get the picture of him out of her mind, his mouth sensuous, his eyes almost black with desire...

"I used to," he corrected gently, reading the memory with disturbing accuracy. "How old were you then? Fifteen?"

She nodded, looking away from him. "Just."

"And I yelled at you, didn't I?" he recalled gently. "I hadn't expected you home. I was hungry and impatient, and frustrated. When I took Jessica home, she was in tears."

"I...I should have knocked," she admitted. "But we'd been to that fair, and I'd won a prize, and I couldn't wait to tell you about it..."

He smiled quietly. "You used to bring all your triumphs straight to me, like a puppy with its toys. Until that night." He studied her averted profile. "You've kept a wall between us ever since. The minute I start to come close, you find something else to put up in front of you. Last time it was Jack Harris. Now, it's that writer."

"I'm not trying to build any walls," she said defensively. Her dark eyes accused him. "You're the mason, Blake. You won't let me be independent."

"What do you want?" he asked.

She studied the delicate scrollwork of the fireplace with its beige and white color scheme. "I don't know," she murmured. "But I'll never find out if you keep smothering me. I want to be free, Blake."

"None of us are that," he said philosophically. His eyes were wistful, his tone bitter. He stared at her intently. "What is it that attracts you to Donavan?" he asked suddenly.

She shrugged and a wistful light came into her own eyes, echoing his expression the minute before. "He's fun to be with. He makes me laugh."

"That's all you need from a man—laughter?"

The way he said it made shivers run down her stiff spine, and when she looked at him, the expression on his hard face was puzzling. "What else is there?" she asked without thinking.

A slow, sensuous smile turned up the corners of his mouth. "The fires a man and woman can create when they make love."

She shifted restlessly in her chair. "They're overrated," she said with pretended sophistication.

He threw back his head and roared.

"Hush!" she said. "You'll wake the whole house!"

His white, even teeth were visible, whiter than ever against his swarthy complexion. "You're red as a summer beet," he observed. "What do you know about love, little girl? You'd pass out in a dead faint if a man started making love to you."

She stared at him with a sense of outrage. "How do you know? Maybe Lawrence..."

"...maybe not," he interrupted, his eyes confident, wise. "You're still very much a virgin, little Kate. If I'd had any fears on that account, I'd have jerked you off Crete so fast your head would have spun."

She grimaced. "Virginity isn't such a prize these days," she sighed, remembering Missy Donavan's faintly insulting remarks about it.

His silent appraisal lasted so long that her attention was caught by the faint ticking of the big grandfather clock in the hall. "Don't get any ideas about throwing yours away," he warned softly.

"Oh, Blake, don't be so old fashioned," she grumbled. "Anyway," she added with a faint, mischievous smile, "where would you be today if all the women in the world were pure?"

"Rather frustrated," he conceded. "But you're not one of my women, and I don't want you offering yourself to men like a nymphomaniac."

She sighed. "There's hardly any danger of that," she said dully. "I don't know how."

"That dress is a damned good start," he observed.

She glanced down at it. "But it covers me up," she protested. "It's a lot more modest than what Nan was wearing."

"I noticed," he said with a musing smile.

She peeked at him through her lashes. "Nan thinks you're the sexiest man alive," she said lightly. "She knew you'd be at the party."

His face hardened. "Nan's a child," he growled turning away with one hand rammed in his pocket. "And I'm too old to encourage hero worship."

Nan was Kathryn's age, exactly. Her heart seemed to plummet, and she wanted to hit out at him. He always made her feel so gauche and ignorant.

She studied his broad back. He was so good to look at. So big and vibrant, and full of life. A quiet man, a caring man. And a tyrant!

"If you won't let me invite Larry here," she murmured, "I suppose I could fly down to the coast and go to that writers' convention with him."

He turned, staring at her, hard and intimidating even at a distance. "Threatening me, Kate?" he asked.

"I wouldn't dare!" she replied fervently.

His dark face was as unreadable as a stone sculpture. "We'll talk about it again."

She scowled at him. "Tyrant," she grumbled.

"Is that your best shot?" he asked politely.

"Male chauvinist!" she said, trying again. "You do irritate me, Blake!"

He moved toward her lazily. "What do you think you do to me, little Kathryn?" he asked, his voice a low growl.

She looked up into his arrogant face as he came within striking distance. "I probably irritate you just as much," she admitted, sighing. "Pax?"

He smiled down at her indulgently. "Pax. Come here."

He tilted her chin up and bent his head down. She closed her eyes, expecting the familiar brief, rough touch of his mouth. But it didn't come.

Puzzled, she opened her eyes and looked straight into his at an unnerving distance. She was so close that she could see the flecks of gold in his dark brown irises, the tiny crinkled lines at the corner of his eyelids.

His fingers touched the side of her throat, warm and strangely caressing.

"Blake?" she whispered uncertainly.

His jaw tautened. She could see a muscle jerk beside his sensuous mouth.

"Welcome home, Kate," he said roughly, and started to move away.

"Aren't you going to kiss me?" she asked without thinking.

All the expression drained out of his face to leave his eyes smoldering as they looked down into hers. "It's late," he said abruptly, turning away, "and I'm tired. Good night, Kate."

He walked out the door and left her standing there, staring at the empty doorway.

Three

Blake was strangely reserved for the next few days, and Kathryn found herself watching him for no reason at all. He was just Blake, she kept telling herself. Just her guardian, as familiar as the towering old house and its ring of live oaks. But something was different. Something ... and she couldn't quite grasp what.

"Blake, are you angry with me?" she asked him one evening as he started upstairs to dress for a date.

He scowled down at her. "What makes you think that, Kathryn?" he asked.

She shrugged, and forced a smile for him. "You seem . . . remote."

"I've got a lot on my mind, kitten," he said quietly.

"The strike?" she guessed.

"That, and a few other assorted headaches," he agreed. "If you're through asking inane questions, I am on my way out."

"Sorry," she said flippantly, "Heaven forbid that I should keep you from the wheat fields."

"Wheat fields?"

"Where you sow your wild oats, of course," she said with what felt like devastating sophistication as she turned to go back in the living room where Phillip and Maude were talking.

He chuckled softly. "Your slip's showing."

She whirled, grasping her midi-length velveteen skirt and staring down at her shapely calf. "Where?"

He went on up the stairs with a low chuckle and she glared after him.

Later, she watched him come back downstairs, dressed in a pair of dark slacks with a white silk shirt open at the neck and a tweed jacket that gave him a rakish look. What woman was he taking out, she wondered, and would she know how to appreciate all that dark, vibrant masculinity? Just the sight of him was enough to make Kathryn's pulse race, and involuntarily she thought back to the night of her homecoming party and the strange look in Blake's eyes when he started to kiss her and didn't. That hesitation had puzzled her ever since, although she tried not to think about it too much. Blake would be frighteningly dangerous in any respect other than that of a cherished adopted brother.

Nan Barrington came over early the next morning to go riding with Kathryn. Petite and fragile-looking in her jodhpurs, she was wearing a blue sweater, very tight, that was the exact shade of her eyes.

She brushed by Kathryn with a tiny sigh, her eyes immediately on everything in sight as she searched the area for Blake.

"He's gone out," Kathryn said with an amused smile.

Nan looked wildly disappointed. "Oh," she said, her face falling. "I just thought he might be going with us."

Kathryn didn't bother to mention that Blake was doing everything short of joining a monastery to avoid her. That would have led to questions she didn't want to face, much less answer.

"Well, there she is, the golden girl," Phillip said from the staircase, gazing with exaggerated interest at the petite blonde. "You luscious creature, you."

Nan laughed delightedly. "Oh, Phil, you're such a tease," she said. "Come riding with us and let me prove that I can still beat the socks off you."

He made a mock pose. "No girl exposes my naked ankles," he scoffed. "You're on!"

Kathryn led them out the door, tugging her green velveteen blouse down over her trim hips as she went, delighting in its warmth in the chill morning air. "It's nippy out here," she murmured. Her slender hand went up to test the strength of the pins that held the coiled rope of hair in place on top of her head. The wind was brisk, invigorating.

"Nice and cool," Phillip agreed. "Strange how Blake's run out of time to ride," he mentioned with a curious glance at Kathryn. "He's literally worked every minute he's been home. And with the Leedses arriving Saturday, he's going to be lucky if he can manage time to pick them up at the airport."

"Fighting again?" Nan probed, shooting a glance at Kathryn.

Kathryn lifted her head and watched the path in front of her as they took the old shortcut to the big barn, with its white-fenced paddocks. The path led through a maze of high, clipped hedges, in the center of which was a white gazebo, carefully concealed, and ringed all the way around with comfortable cushions. Kathryn had always thought it a wildly romantic setting, and her imagination ran riot every time she saw it.

"Blake and I are getting along just fine," she said, denying her friend's teasing accusation.

"Nothing easier," Phillip agreed with a grin. "They never see each other."

"We do," Kathryn disagreed. "Remember the other night when Blake was going out on that date?"

Nan glanced up at Phillip. "Who's he after now?" She laughed.

Phillip shrugged fatalistically. "Who knows? I think it's the little blonde he's got in the office. His new secretary, if office gossip can be believed. But I hear she can't spell cat."

"Blake likes blondes, all right." Kathryn laughed with an amusement that she was far from feeling.

"Here's one he sure avoids," Nan groaned. "What's wrong with me?"

Phillip threw an avuncular arm across her shoulders. "Your age, my dear," he informed her. "Blake likes his women mature, sophisticated and thoroughly immoral. That leaves you out of the running."

Nan sighed miserably. "I always have been."

"Blake used to pick us up after cheerleading practice, remember," Kathryn said, eyeing the gazebo longingly as they passed it. "He still thinks of us chewing bubble gum and giggling."

"I hate bubble gum," Nan pouted.

"So do I," Phillip agreed. "It leaves a bad...well, hello," he broke off, grinning at Blake.

The older man stopped in their path, dressed in a sophisticated gray business suit, with a spotless white silk shirt and a patterned tie. He looked every inch the business magnate, polished and dignified.

"Good morning," Blake said coolly. He smiled at Nan. "How's your mother?"

"Just fine, Blake," Nan sighed, going close to catch his arm in her slender fingers. "Don't you have time to go riding with us?"

"I wish I did, little one," he told her. "But I'm already late for a conference."

Kathryn turned away and started for the barn. "I'm going ahead," she called over her shoulder. "Last one in the saddle's a greenhorn!"

She almost ran the rest of the way to the barn, shocked at her own behavior. She felt strange. Sick. Hurt. Empty. The sight of Nan clinging to Blake's arm had set off a rage within her. She'd wanted to slap her friend of many years, just for touching him. She didn't understand herself at all.

Absently, she went into the tackroom and started getting together bits and bridles and a saddle. She barely noticed when the lithe chestnut gelding was saddled and ready to mount. He pranced nervously, as if he sensed her uneasy mood and was reacting to it.

Nan joined her as she was leading Sundance out into the bright morning.

"Where's Phil?" Kathryn asked, trying to keep the edge out of her voice.

Nan shrugged curiously. "Blake dragged him off to the office for some kind of council of war. At least, that's what it sounded like." She sighed. "Blake seemed very angry with him." Her face brightened. "Almost as if he didn't like the idea of Phillip going riding with me. Kate, do you suppose he's jealous?" she asked excitedly.

"It wouldn't surprise me a bit," Kathryn lied, remembering Blake's remarks about her friend. But, frowning, she couldn't help wondering if he'd meant it. Why in the world didn't he want Phillip to ride with the girls?

Kathryn knew that Blake felt Phillip's attitude toward the multi-company enterprise was a little slack sometimes. But why drag him off at this hour of the morning unless... She didn't want to think about it. If Nan was right, she didn't want to know.

"Get saddled and let's go!" Kathryn called. "I'm itching for a gallop!"

"Why did you run off back there?" Nan asked before she went into the stable to saddle her mount.

"Do hurry," Kathryn said, ignoring the question. "Maude wants me to help her plan some menus for the Leedses' visit."

Nan hurriedly saddled her mount, a little mare with the unlikely name of Whirlwind, and the disposition of a sunny summer day.

The two girls rode in a companionable silence, and Kathryn gazed lovingly at the rolling green hills in their autumn colors, trees in the distance just beginning to don the soft golds that later would become brilliant oranges and reds and burgundy. The air was clean and fresh, and fields beyond the meadows were already being turned over to wait for spring planting.

"Isn't it delicious?" Kathryn breathed. "South Carolina must be the most beautiful state in the country."

"You only say that because you're a native," Nan teased.

"It's true, though." She reined in and leaned forward, crossing her forearms on the pommel to stare at the silver ribbon of the Edisto River beyond.

"Do you know how many rice plantations there were in Charleston just before the Civil War?" she murmured, remembering books she'd read about those great plantations with their neat square fields and floodgates.

"I'm afraid I don't share your passion for history, Kate," Nan said apologetically. "Sometimes I even forget what year they fought the War of 1812."

Kathryn smiled at her friend, and all the resentment drained out of her. After all, Nan couldn't help the way she felt about Blake. It wasn't her fault he was so wickedly attractive...

"Let's ride down through the woods," she said abruptly, wheeling Sundance. "I love to smell the river, don't you?"

"Oh, yes," Nan agreed. "I'm with you!"

Blake was home for dinner that night, an occurrence rare enough to cause comment.

"Run out of girls?" Phillip teased as they sat around the table nibbling at Mrs. Johnson's chicken casserole.

"Phillip!" Maude chided, her dark eyes disapproving as she paused in the act of lifting a forkful of chicken to her mouth.

Blake raised an eyebrow at his brother. His blue-checked sports shirt was open at the neck, and he looked vibrant and rested and dangerously attractive to Kathryn, who was doing her best to keep her eyes away from him.

"You had more than your share this morning," Blake remarked dryly.

"Was that why you dragged me off to the office before I could enjoy being surrounded by them?" Phillip laughed.

"I needed your support, little brother."

"Sure. The way Samson needed a herd of horses to help him tug the pillars down."

"I would like to point out," Maude said gently, "That Mrs. Johnson spent an hour preparing this excellent chicken dish, which is turning to bile in my stomach."

Kathryn darted an amused glance at the older woman. "You should have had daughters," she suggested.

Maude stared at Blake, then at Phillip. "I'm not sure. It's very hard to picture Blake in spike heels and a petticoat."

Kathryn choked on her mashed potatoes, and Phillip had to lean over and thump her on the back.

"I'm glad Kathryn finds something amusing," Blake said in that cold, curt tone that she hated so much. "She wasn't in the best of humors this morning."

Kathryn swallowed a sip of coffee, and her dark green eyes glared at Blake across the table. "I don't remember saying anything to you at all, Blake," she murmured.

"No," he agreed. "You were too busy flouncing off to offer a civil greeting."

How could he be so blind? she wondered, but she only glared at him. "Excuse me," she said haughtily, "but I never flounce."

He lifted his coffee cup to his chiseled lips, but his eyes never left Kathryn's face. Something dark and hard in them unnerved her. "Push a little harder, honey," he challenged quietly.

Her small frame stiffened. "I'm not afraid of you," she said with a forced smile.

His eyes narrowed, and a corner of his mouth went up. "I could teach you to be," he said.

"Now, children," Maude began, her eyes plainly indicating which of the two she was referring to as they glared at Kathryn. "This is the meal hour, remember? Indigestion is bad for the soul."

Phillip sighed as he tasted his lemon mousse. "It's never stopped them before," he muttered.

Kathryn crumpled her napkin and laid it beside her plate before she got to her feet. "I think I'll play the piano for a while, if no one minds."

"Not for too long, dear, you'll keep Blake awake," Maude cautioned. "Remember, he has to get up at five in the morning to drive down to Charleston to pick up the Leedses at the airport.''

Kathryn threw a gracious smile in Blake's direction. "Of course," she said with honey in her voice. "Our elders must have their beauty rest."

"By heaven, you're asking for it," Blake said in a voice that sent chills down her spine.

"Go, girl!" Phillip said, pushing her in the direction of the living room. He closed the door behind them with an exaggerated sigh and leaned against it. "Whew!" he breathed, and his dark eyes laughed at her when he opened them again. "Don't push your luck, sweet. He's been impossible to get along with for days now, and this morning he made a barracuda look tame."

"Doesn't he always?" she grumbled.

"Yes," he conceded. "But if you had his secretary, it might give you ulcers as well."

She glanced at him as she went to the piano and sat down, flexing her fingers. "If he wants secretaries who decorate instead of type, that's his business. Just hush, Phil, will you? I'm sick of hearing about Blake!"

She banged away at Rachmaninoff's Second Piano Concerto, while Phillip stared at her profile thoughtfully for a long time.

Four

Maude had the housekeeper, buxom Mrs. Johnson, and the two little daily maids running in circles by late afternoon. It was almost comical, and Kathryn had to force herself not to giggle.

"Don't put the urn of dried flowers *there,*" Maude wailed when one of the maids placed it in the entrance to the living room.

Kathryn decided she had better go outside and keep out of the way.

Phillip was just getting out of his small sports car as she emerged from the house. He hesitated for an instant when he saw Kathryn coming, then got the rest of the way out and closed the door.

"What's the matter with you?" he asked cheerfully.

"It's the dried flowers," she explained enigmatically.

Phillip blinked. "Have you been into Blake's whiskey, Kathryn?"

She shook her head. "You had to be there to understand," she told him. "Honestly, you'd think the head of state was coming. She's rearranged the furniture twice, and now she's going crazy over flowers. And just think, Phil," she added in a conspiratorial whisper, "Leeds can't even save the river!"

He chuckled. "Probably not. Blake should be back soon," he said, after a glance at his watch.

Kathryn looked out over the sculptured garden with its cobblestone path leading through hedges to the concealed white gazebo. "I wonder what Miss Leeds looks like?" she murmured thoughtfully.

"Vivian?" he asked, smiling. "The cover of a fashion magazine. She's an actress, you know, quite well-known already, too."

She felt ill. "Old?" she asked.

"Twenty-five isn't old, sweet." He laughed. "Blake can't be without a woman for long. He really can pick them."

She wanted to hit him. To scream. To do anything but stand there with a calm smile plastered to her face and pretend it didn't matter. Suddenly, terribly, it mattered. Blake was her... She stopped, frowning. Her *what?*

"Kathryn, you aren't listening," Phillip said patiently. "I said, would you like to go into King's Fort with me and buy a new dress or two?"

She looked up at him. "Whatever for?" she asked indignantly. "I don't dress in rags!"

"Of course not," he said, placating her. "But Maude suggested that you might like some new clothes since we're having guests."

She drew a deep, angry breath. "Put on my best feathers, you mean?" She thought about it, imagining an outfit daring enough to make even Blake take notice. A tiny smile touched her pink mouth. "All right. Take me someplace expensive. Saks, I think."

"Uh, Kathryn..." Phillip said.

"Blake won't get the bill until next month," she reminded him. "By then, I can be in St. Martin, or Tahiti, or Paris..."

He chuckled. "All right, incorrigible girl, come on. We've got to hurry or we won't be here when Blake's guests arrive."

Kathryn didn't tell him, but that was just what she had in mind. The idea of greeting Vivian Leeds made her want to spend several days in town. She disliked the woman already, and she hadn't even met her.

She left Phillip in a small, exotic coffee shop on the mall while she floated through the plush women's department in the exclusive shop, dreaming of Blake seeing her in one expensive dress after another. She'd show him! She'd be the most beautiful woman he'd ever seen, and she'd make him stand back and take notice!

But when she tried on one of the elegant dresses she'd picked out, all she saw in the mirror was a little girl trying to play dress-up. She looked about fifteen. All the excitement drained out of her face. Her whole body seemed to slump as she stared at her reflection.

"It doesn't suit you, does it?" the pleasant blond saleswoman asked her.

Kathryn shook her head sadly. "It looked so beautiful on the model..."

"Because it was designed for a taller, thinner figure than yours," the statuesque older woman explained. "If I may suggest some styles...?"

"Oh, please!" Kathryn said, wide-eyed.

"Wait here."

The three dresses the woman brought back looked far less dramatic than those Kathryn had picked out. They were simple garments with no frills at all, and the colors were pale pastels—mint, taupe and a silky beige. But on Kathryn, they came to life. Combined with her black hair and green eyes, the mint was devastating. The taupe emphasized her rounded figure and darkened her eyes. The beige brought out her soft complexion and its simple lines gave her an elegance far beyond her years.

"And this is for evening," the woman said at last, bringing out a burgundy velvet gown with a deep V-neck and slits down both sides. It's a dream of a dress, Kathryn thought, studying her reflection in the mirror, her face glowing as she imagined Blake's reaction to this seductive style—the light went out of her suddenly when she remembered the warning he'd given her, about provoking him. But surely she had the right to wear what she pleased . . .

"Kathryn, we've got to go," Phillip called to her.

One expressive eyebrow went up, and her eyes danced mischievously. What would this gorgeous gown do to Phillip?

She opened the curtains and walked out. He stared at her, with lips slightly parted, his brown eyes stunned.

"Kathryn?" he asked, as if he didn't trust his eyes anymore.

"Yes, it's me," she assured him. "Oh, Phil, isn't it a dream?"

He nodded dubiously. "A dream."

"What's the matter?" she asked, going close to look up at him, while the saleswoman smiled secretively from a distance.

"Are you sure it's legal to wear something like that in public?" he asked.

She smiled. "Why not? It's very fashionable. Do you really like it?"

He caught his breath. "Honey, I love it. But Blake..."

She glared at him. "I'm grown. I keep having to remind Blake..."

"You won't have to remind him anymore if you wear that dress," he said, staring down at the soft, exposed curves of her breasts in the plunging neckline. "He'll be able to see for himself."

She tossed her long, waving hair defiantly. "I'll bet that actress wears more revealing clothes than this."

"She does," he agreed, "but her lifestyle is different from yours, kitten."

"You mean she sleeps with men, don't you, Phillip?" she persisted.

"Hush, for heaven's sake!" he said quickly, looking around to see if anyone was listening. "Remember where we are."

"But she does, doesn't she?" she kept on, glaring.

"I know you've been at it with Blake about your writer friend coming," Phillip told her quietly. "But don't think you'll retaliate by insulting his latest female acquisition. He'll cut you into little pieces, Kate."

She felt the rage welling up in her like rain catching in a vat. "I'm tired of Blake telling me how to live my life. I want to move into an apartment."

"Don't tell him yet," Phillip pleaded.

"I already have," she replied, her eyes sparkling with temper.

"And what did he say?"

"He said no, of course. He always says no. But it won't work anymore. I'm going to get a job, and an apartment, and you're going to help me," she added, with a mischievous glance upward.

"Oh, like hell I am!" he replied. "I'm not taking on Blake for you."

She stamped her small foot. "That's what's wrong with men today!"

His eyebrows went up amusedly. "What is?"

"That no one's brave enough to take on Blake for me! I'll bet Larry will," she added stubbornly.

"If he does, he'll wish he hadn't," Phillip said. "And if you buy that dress, Kathryn, I'm going away for the weekend." He made a mock shudder. "I can't stand the sight of blood."

"Blake won't do anything," she said smugly. "Not in front of his guests."

"Blake will do anything, anytime, in front of anybody, and if you don't know that by now, you're even crazier than I thought you were." He shook his head. "Give it up, Kathy. Blake's only trying to do what's best for you."

"That's beside the point, Phillip," she replied, smoothing the velvet under her slender fingers. "I don't want to spend the rest of my life being told what to do. Blake's not my keeper."

"If you go out after dark in that dress, you'll need one," he murmured, staring at her.

She leaned up and kissed his cheek. "You're a nice man."

"Kathryn, are you sure . . . ?"

"Don't be such a worrywart," she told him. She motioned to the saleswoman. "I'll take all of them," she said with a smile. "And that green velvet one, as well."

Phillip frowned. "What green velvet one?"

"It's ever so much more daring than this," she lied, remembering the high halter neckline and soft lines of the other dress she'd tried on. "It doesn't have a back at all," she added in a wicked whisper.

"Lord help us!" Phillip said, lifting his eyes upward.

"Don't bother Him," Kate said, "He has wars and floods to worry about."

"And I have you," he groaned.

"Lucky man," she said, patting his cheek before she went to charge her purchases. "Come on. You have to sign the ticket."

"Whose name would you like me to sign on it?" he asked.

"Oh, silly!" she laughed.

She and Phillip had managed to sneak in the back way and dart upstairs to dress for dinner without being seen. Recklessly, Kathryn slid into the burgundy velvet dress after she had her bath, and tacked up her long hair in a seductively soft bun on top of her head with little curling wisps trailing down her blushing cheeks. She used only a little makeup—just enough to give her a mysterious look, a hint of sophistication. The woman looking back at her in the mirror bore no resemblance to the young girl who'd left that room the same day to go shopping.

Satisfied with what she saw, she added a touch of Givenchy perfume and sauntered downstairs. She heard voices coming from the living room, and Blake's was among them. She felt suddenly nervous, uneasy. That would never do. She lifted her head, baring the soft curve of her throat, and, gathering her courage, walked straight into the white-carpeted, blue-furnished room.

She noticed two things immediately: the possessive blonde clinging to Blake's sleeve like a parasite, and the sudden, blazing fury in Blake's eyes as he looked at Kathryn Mary.

"Oh, there you are, darl...ing," Maude said, her voice breaking on the word as she noticed the dress. "How...different you look, Kathryn," she added with a disapproving glance.

"Where did you get that dress?" Blake asked in a harsh, low voice.

She started to speak, then darted a glance at Phillip, who was burying his face in his hand. "Phillip bought it for me," she said in a rush.

"Kathryn!" Phillip groaned.

Blake smiled, like a hungry barracuda, Kathryn thought shakily. "I'll discuss this with you later, Phil."

"Could we make it after Kathryn's funeral?" Phillip asked, with a meaningful glance at Kathryn.

"Aren't you going to introduce me to your guests?" Kathryn asked brightly.

"Dick Leeds and his daughter, Vivian," Blake said, indicating a tall, white-haired man with twinkling blue eyes and the equally blue-eyed blonde at Blake's side. "This is Kathryn Mary."

"Kilpatrick," she added proudly. "I'm the youngest, next to Phillip."

"How do you do?" Dick Leeds asked pleasantly, and extended a thin hand to be shook. He smiled at her. "Not a Hamilton, then?" he asked.

"I'm a cousin," she explained. "Maude and the family took me in when my parents died, and brought me up."

"Apparently not too successfully," Blake said darkly, his eyes promising retribution as they seared a path down her body, lingering on the plunging neckline.

"If you don't stop picking on me, Blake," she said sweetly, accepting a glass of sherry from Phillip, "I'll hit you with my teddy bear."

Vivian Leeds didn't look amused, although her lips managed a thin smile. "How old are you, Miss Kilpatrick?" she asked listlessly.

"Much younger than you, Miss Leeds, I'm sure," Kathryn replied with an equally false smile.

Phillip choked on his drink. "Uh, how was your trip, Viv?" he asked the blonde, quickly.

"Very nice, thanks," she replied, her eyes cutting a hole in Kathryn. "Lovely dress," she said. "What there is of it."

"This old rag?" Kathryn said haughtily, her eyes speaking volumes as they studied the rose silk gown the blonde was wearing. "It's warm, at least," she added. "I don't really care for these new fashions— some of them look more like nighties than dresses," she said pointedly.

Miss Leeds's face colored expressively, her blue eyes lighting like firecrackers.

"Let's eat," Maude said suddenly.

"Lead the way, Mother," Blake said. Amusement was vying with anger in his dark eyes, and just for an instant, amusement won. But then his dark gaze slid sideways to Kathryn, and the smile faded. His eyes curved over the creamy, exposed skin at her neckline, and she felt as if he had touched her. Her lips parted under a rush of breath, and he looked up suddenly and caught that expression on her young face. Something flared in his dark eyes, like a minor volcanic upheaval, and Kathryn knew that she was going to be in the middle of a war before the night was over. But she managed to return Blake's glare with bravado, and even smiled. If she was going to be the main course on his menu, she might as well enjoy the appetizer first.

Phillip dropped back beside her as they made their way into the dining room. "Feeling suicidal?" he asked under his breath. "He's blazing, and that sweet little smile didn't help."

"Revolutionaries can't afford to worry about tomorrow," she replied saucily. "Besides, Blake can't eat me."

"Can't he?" he asked, casting a wary glance toward his brother, who was glaring at them over Vivian's bright head.

"Phillip, you aren't really afraid of him, are you?" she teased. "After all, you're brothers."

"So," he reminded her, "were Cain and Abel."

"Don't worry, I'll protect you."

"Please don't," he asked mournfully. "Why did you have to tell him that I bought you that dress?"

"But, you did sign for it," she said innocently.

"I know, but buying it wasn't my idea."

"Be reasonable, Phil," she said soothingly. "If I'd told him it was my idea, he'd have gone straight for my throat."

He gave her a measuring look. "And having him go for mine was a better idea?"

She smiled. "From my point of view, it was," she laughed. "Oh, Phil, I am sorry, really I am. I'll tell him the truth."

"If you get the chance," he muttered under his breath, nodding toward his brother.

Blake seated Vivian and then turned to hold out a chair for Kathryn. She approached it with the same aplomb as a condemned terrorist headed for the gallows.

"Nice party," she murmured under her breath as she sat down.

"And it's only beginning," he said with a smile that didn't reach his eyes. "Make one more snide remark to Vivian, and I'll grind you into the carpet, Kathryn Mary."

She spared him a cool glance. "She started it," she said under her breath.

"Jealous?" he taunted softly.

Her eyes jerked up to his, blazing green fire. "Of her?" she asked haughtily. "I'm not fifteen anymore," she said.

"Before the night's over, you're going to wish you were," he said softly. "I promise you."

The deep anger in his voice sent chills running all over her. Why did she have to open her mouth and challenge him again? Hadn't she had enough warning? She felt a surge of fear at what lay ahead. It seemed that she couldn't stop fighting Blake lately, and she wondered at her own temerity. Was she going mad?

One glance at his set face down the table from her was enough to make her want to run upstairs and bar the door.

Dinner was an ordeal. Vivian monopolized Blake to such an extent that he was hardly able to carry on a conversation with anyone else, but her cold blue eyes made frequent pilgrimages to Kathryn's quiet face. The animosity in them was freezing.

"You're not doing much for international relations," Phillip remarked as they retired to the living room for after-dinner drinks.

"Blake's doing enough for both of us," she replied, darting a cool glance toward the blonde, who was clinging to Blake's big, muscular arm as if he were a life raft. "He has bad taste," she said without thinking.

"I wouldn't say that," Phillip disagreed. His brown eyes danced as they surveyed the blonde's graceful back. "She's pretty easy on the eyes."

"Is she?" she asked with magnificent disdain. "Frankly, she doesn't do a thing for me."

"Don't be sour," he said. "You forget why she's here, darling. Remember the strike?"

"Oh, I remember," she told him. "But does Blake? I thought her father was the focal point."

"Part of it, at least," he said.

She stared up at him. "What do you mean, Phil?" she asked curiously.

He avoided her sharp eyes. "You'll know soon enough. Look, Mother's motioning to you."

Maude was showing some of her antique frames to Dick Leeds, but she left him with a smile and drew Kathryn aside.

"You're doing it again, my darling," she moaned, darting a wary glance in Blake's direction. "He's ready to chew nails. Kathryn, can't you manage not to antagonize him for just one evening? The Leedses are our guests, remember."

"They're Blake's guests," came the sullen reply.

"Well, it is Blake's house," Maude said with a placating smile. "Johnny left it all to him. He felt Blake would keep me from frittering it away."

"You wouldn't have," Kathryn protested.

Maude sighed. "Perhaps," she said wistfully. "But it's a moot point. You aren't improving Blake's disposition, you know."

"All I did was buy a new dress," she said defensively.

"It's much too old for you, Kathryn," she said quietly. "Phillip hasn't taken his eyes off you all evening, and every time he looks at you, Blake scowls more.''

''Phillip and I aren't related, after all,'' Kathryn pointed out.

Maude smiled. ''And there's no one I'd rather see him marry, you know that. But Blake doesn't approve, and he could make things very difficult for you.''

She scowled. ''He doesn't approve of any man I date,'' she grumbled.

Maude started to say something, but obviously thought better of it. ''It will work itself out. Meanwhile, please at least be civil to Miss Leeds. It's terribly important that we make a good impression on them both. I can't tell you any more than that, but do trust me.''

Kathryn sighed. ''I will.''

Maude patted Kathryn's slender shoulder. ''Now be a dear, and help me entertain Dick. Blake is going to drive Vivian into King's Fort and show her how the city looks at night. She was curious, for some reason that escapes me.''

It didn't escape Kathryn, and it didn't improve her mood, either. Especially when she watched Vivian and Blake go out the door without a backward glance. She wanted to pick up the priceless Tang dynasty vase in the hall and heave it at Blake's dark head. In the end, she consoled herself with the fact that at least she didn't have to face Blake until the morning. That was a blessing in itself.

Dick Leeds was interesting to talk to. She liked the elderly man, who seemed to have the same kind of steel in his makeup that Blake did. All too soon, he went upstairs to his room, pleading fatigue from the long trip. Maude followed suit with a sigh.

"Like Dick," she told Phillip and Kathryn, "I'm beginning to feel my age a little. Good night, children."

Phillip challenged Kathryn to a game of gin rummy after Maude went out the door, but she protested.

"You'll just beat me again," she pouted.

"I'll give myself a ten-point handicap," he promised.

"Well . . . just a couple of hands," she agreed finally.

He held out a chair for her at the small table by the darkened window. "Sit down, pigeon . . . I mean, partner," he grinned.

She smiled across the table at him. "Why can't Blake be like you?" she wondered absently as he shuffled the cards. "Friendly, and easy to get along with, and fun to be around . . ."

"He used to be, when you were younger," he answered, and his warm brown eyes twinkled. "It's only since you've started growing up that you think he's changed."

She stuck out her tongue at him. "I don't think, I know! He growls at me all the time."

"You light the fires under him, my sweet. Like tonight."

Her face closed up, like a fragile flower in a sudden chill. "I don't like her."

"And the feeling seems to be mutual. I don't think attractive women ever really like each other." He studied her unobtrusively. "But I have an idea that her dislike stems from your own. You've hardly been friendly toward her."

She drew in a defeated sigh. "You're right, I haven't," she admitted.

"Trying to get back at Blake?" he persisted.

"My arsenal is limited when it comes to fighting your brother," she sighed.

He laid down three cards in sequence and discarded. "That goes for all of us."

She held the cool cards up to her lips absently while she drew a card, looked at it, grimaced, and laid it down on the discard pile. "I don't see why I can't have an apartment," she said. Her full lips pouted against the cards. "I can get a job and pay for it."

"A job doing what?" he asked politely.

She glared at him. "That's the problem. Finishing school didn't prepare me for much of anything. I know," she said, brightening. "I'll advertise to be a rich man's mistress! I'm eminently qualified for that!"

Phillip buried his face in his hands. "Don't you dare say that to Blake when I'm in the room! He'll think I suggested it!"

She laughed at the expression on his face. Phillip was such fun, and such a gentleman. She was fonder of him than she liked to say. He was truly like the brother she wished she'd had. But Blake...she turned her attention back to her cards.

She was so caught up in the game of gin rummy that she forgot the time. She was one card short of winning the game when all of a sudden she heard the front door open and she froze in her seat.

"Oops," she murmured weakly.

Phillip smothered a grin at the look on her soft features. "Sounds like they're home," he commented, as Vivian's high-pitched voice called goodnight from the staircase.

Before she could reply, Blake, looking big, dark and formidable, came in the door. He glanced at the tableau they made as he slung his jacket onto a chair and tugged his tie loose, tossing it carelessly onto the jacket.

"Have a good time?" Phillip asked slyly, his sharp gaze not missing the smear of lipstick just visible on Blake's shirt collar.

Blake shrugged. He went to the bar and poured himself a jigger of whiskey, neat.

"Uh, I think I'd better get to bed," Phillip said, gauging Blake's mood with lightning precision. "Good night, all."

"I think I'll go up, too," Kathryn began hopefully, rising as Phillip made his hasty exit and disappeared into the hall.

Kathryn was only a step behind him when Blake's curt voice stopped her with her hand on the doorknob.

"Close the door," he said.

She started to go through it.

"From the inside," he added in a tone that was honeyed, yet vaguely threatening.

She drew a steadying breath and went back into the living room, closing the door reluctantly behind her. She leaned back against it, flashing a nervous glance at him.

"Did you have a nice drive?" she asked.

"Don't hedge," he growled. His angry eyes slid down her body in the velvet dress with its side slits and plunging neckline, and she felt as if his hands were touching her bare flesh.

"Dick's gone to bed. He's very nice," she murmured, trying to postpone the confrontation as long as possible. She'd seen Blake in plenty of bad tempers, but judging by the control she read in his face, this one was formidable. The courage she'd felt earlier, in company, dissolved now that she was alone with him.

"So is his daughter," he replied. "Not that you've taken the trouble to find out."

She shifted against the cold wood at her back. "She bites."

"So do you, honey," he replied, lifting his glass to his lips. "I want the truth, Kate. Did Phillip buy you that dress?"

She felt weary all of a sudden, defeated. Blake always seemed to win. "No," she admitted. "That is, he signed for it because I don't have a charge account, but Maude said herself that I needed some new clothes," she added defensively.

"I said the same thing. But I hadn't planned on your dressing like a Main Street prostitute."

"It's the style, Blake!" she shot at him.

"Almost exactly the same words you used after the Barringtons' party," he reminded her. "And I told you the same thing then that I'm telling you now. A dress like that raises a man's blood pressure by five points while it's still on the mannequin. On you..." He let his eyes speak for him, dark and sensuous as they caressed her.

"Vivian was wearing less," she replied weakly, feeling the heat in her cheeks. "I could almost see through *her* dress."

"Throwing stones?" he asked. "Your breasts are barely covered at all."

Her face went hot under the words, and she glared at him with outrage in her sparkling green eyes. "Oh, all right, I'll never wear the silly dress again, Blake! But I can't see what difference it makes to you what I wear!"

His eyes narrowed, and his hand tightened on the thick glass. "Can't you?"

She squared her small shoulders. "You're just being a tyrant again," she accused. Her hands slid down the sensuous burgundy velvet over her hips as she lifted her face defiantly. "What's the matter, Blake, do I disturb you?" she challenged. "Would you rather I wore my gym suit from high school?"

He set the glass down on the bar and strode toward her deliberately, his eyes blazing, his face

harder than granite. She saw the purpose in his eyes
and turned with a feeling of panic, grabbing for the
doorknob. But the action was too late. He caught her
and whirled her around with rough, hurting hands to
hold her, struggling against the door.

Five

She stared up into the face of a stranger, and her voice caught in her throat. "Blake, you wouldn't...!" she burst out finally, frightened by what she read in his dark eyes.

He moved, and his big, warm body crushed her against the door. She felt the pressure of his hard, powerful thighs against hers, the metal of his belt buckle sharp at her stomach. There was the rustle of cloth against cloth as his hands caught her bare arms and stilled her struggles.

"Oh, wouldn't I?" he growled, as his eyes dropped to her tremulous lips.

Stunned by the sight of his dark, leonine face at such a disturbing proximity, she looked up at him helplessly until he suddenly crushed her soft mouth under his, forcing her head back under the merciless pressure.

She kept her mouth tightly closed, her body trembling with sudden fear at what Blake was asking of her. She stiffened, struggling instinctively, and his mouth twisted against hers to hold it in bondage, his teeth nipping her lower lip painfully.

A sob broke from her tight throat as she yielded to the merciless ardor that was years beyond her few experiences with men. Nothing that had gone before prepared her for the adult passion she felt in Blake, and it sparked a response that was mingled fear and shock. This was no boyfriend assaulting her senses. This was Blake. Blake, who taught her to ride. Blake, who drove her to cheerleading practice and football games with her friend Nan. Blake, who was a confidant, a protector, and now...

He jerked his head up suddenly, surveying the damage in her swollen, bruised lips, her wounded eyes, her wildly flushed cheeks and disordered hair.

"You're...hurting me," she whispered brokenly. Her fingers went to her drooping coiffure, nervously, as tears washed her eyes.

His face seemed to harden as he looked down at her. His breath came hard and fast. His eyes glittered with unfathomable emotions.

"This is what happens when you throw that sweet young body at me," he said in a voice that cut. "I warned you before about flaunting it, and you wouldn't listen. Now, maybe I've managed to get through to you."

She drew in a sobbing breath, and the tiny sound seemed to disturb him. His eyes softened, just a little, as they wandered over her face.

"Please let me go, Blake," she pleaded in a shaken whisper. "I swear, I'll wear sackcloth and ashes for the rest of my life!"

His heavy brows drew together and he let go of her arms to lean his hands on either side of her head against the door, pushing back a little to ease the crush of his powerful chest and thighs.

"Afraid?" he asked in a deep, lazy voice.

She swallowed hard, nodding, her eyes mesmerized by his.

He let his eyes move down to her swollen, cut lip as he bent toward her again. She felt his tongue brushing very softly against it, healing, tantalizing and she gasped again—but this time, not in pain.

He drew back and caught her eyes. The expression he found was one of curiosity, uncertainty. She met that searching gaze squarely and felt the breath sigh out of her body. Her heart went wild under the intensity of it. She wanted suddenly to reach up and bring his dark head back down again, to feel his mouth again. To open her lips and taste his. To kiss him hungrily, and hard, and feel his body against the length of hers as it had been, but not in anger this time.

His jaw went rigid. His eyes seemed to burst with light and darkness. Then, suddenly, she was free. He pushed away from her and turned to walk back to the bar. He poured himself another whiskey, and paused long enough to dash a jigger of brandy into a snifter for her before he moved back to the door where she stood frozen and handed it to her.

Wordlessly, he caught her free hand and drew her back to his desk with him. He perched against it, holding her in front of him while she nervously sipped the fiery amber liquid.

He threw down his own drink and put first his own glass, then hers, aside. He reached out to catch her by the waist, drawing her gently closer. He stared down at her flushed face for a long time before he spoke, in a silence heady with new emotions.

"Don't brood," he said, in a tone that carried echoes of her childhood. Blake's voice, gentle, soothing her when her world caved in. "The tactics may have been different, but it was only an argument. It's over."

She pretended a calm she didn't feel, and some of the tension went out of her shocked body. "That doesn't sound very much like an apology," she said, darting a shy glance up at him.

One eyebrow lifted. "I'm not going to apologize. You asked for that, Kathryn, and you know it."

She sighed shakily. "I know." Her eyes traced the powerful lines of his chest. "I didn't mean to say what I did."

"All you have to remember, little innocent one," he said indulgently, "is that verbal warfare brings a man's blood up. You can be provocative without even realizing it." He shook her gently. "Are you listening?"

"Yes." Her dark, curious eyes darted up to his for an instant. "You...I didn't think that you..." she stopped, trying to find words.

"There's no blood between us to protect you from me, Kate," he said in a deep, quiet tone. "I'm not in my dotage, and I react like any normal man to the sight of a woman in a revealing dress. Phillip could have lost his head just as easily," he added gruffly.

She felt her heart pounding and caught her breath. "Perhaps," she whispered. "But he would have been...gentle, I think."

He didn't argue the point. His big, warm hand tilted her face up to his quiet eyes. "Another of the many differences between Phillip and me, young Kate," he said. "I'm not a gentle lover. I like my women...practiced."

The flush made bright banners in her cheeks. "Do they get combat pay?" she asked with a hint of impudence and a wry smile as she touched her forefinger gingerly to her cut lip.

His lips turned up, and his dark eyes sparkled. It was as if there had never been a harsh scene to alienate them. "It works both ways, honey," he replied musingly. "Some women would have returned the compliment, with interest."

Her eyes looked deep into his. This, she thought dazedly, is getting interesting. "Women...bite men?" she asked in a whisper, as if it was a subject not fit for decent ears to hear.

"Yes," he whispered back. "And claw, and scream like banshees."

"I...I don't mean *then*," she said. "I mean when...oh, never mind, you just want to make fun of me. I'll ask Phillip."

He chuckled softly. "Do you really think he's ever felt that kind of passion?" he asked.

She shrugged. "He's a man."

"Men are different," he reminded her. His eyes dropped to her mouth. "Poor little scrap, I did hurt you, didn't I?" he asked gently.

She drew away from him, and he relaxed his hold to free her. "It's all right," she murmured. "As you said, I did ask for it." Her eyes glanced off his. "You're . . . very sophisticated."

"And you're a delicious little innocent," he replied. "I didn't mean to be so brutal with you, but I do want to impress on you what you invite from a man with a dress like that." He smiled drily. "I've got a low boiling point, Kate, and I do recall warning you."

"I didn't think you were serious," she said with a sigh.

His dark eyes swept over her again. "Now you know better."

"And better," she agreed. She turned, almost knocking over Maude's priceless porcelain vase on its marble-topped table on the way out. "I'm taking back every dress I bought while there's still time."

"Kate, don't be ridiculous," he growled after her. "You know what I meant. I don't want you wearing dresses with necklines cut to the waist, that's all. You're still too much a child to realize what you could be letting yourself in for."

She turned at the door with great dignity, her carriage so perfect that Mademoiselle Devres would have cheered. "I'm not a child anymore, Blake," she told him. "Am I?"

He turned away, bending his head to light a cigarette with steady hands. "When does that writer get here?"

She swallowed nervously. "Tomorrow morning." She watched him walk to the darkened window and draw the curtain aside to look out. His broad back was toward her and unexpectedly, she remembered how warm and sensuous it had felt under the palms of her hands.

"Aren't you going to tell me to call it off again?" she asked, testing him, feeling a flick of danger run through her that was madly exciting.

He stared at her across the room for a long moment before he answered. "At least I won't have to worry about you sneaking off to go to that convention with him while he's under my roof," he remarked carelessly. "And he'd have his work cut out to seduce you, from what I've seen tonight."

Her eyes flashed at him. "That's what you think!" she shot back.

He only laughed, softly, sensuously. "Before you flounce off, hugging your boundless attractions to your bare bosom, you might remember that I wasn't trying to seduce you. You ought to know by now that my taste doesn't run to oversexed adolescents. Not that you fall in that classification,'' he added with a mocking smile. "You're green for a young woman just shy of her twenty-first birthday."

That hurt, even more than the devastating taste of him as a lover. "Larry doesn't think so," she told him.

He lifted the cigarette to his hard mouth, his eyes laughing at her. "If I had his limited experience, I might agree with him."

That nudged a suspicion in the back of her mind. "What do you know about his experience?" she asked.

He studied her for a long, static silence. "Did you really think I'd let you go to Crete with him and that harebrained sister of his without checking them out thoroughly?"

Her face flamed. "You don't trust me, do you?"

"On the contrary, I trust you implicitly. But I don't trust men," he said arrogantly.

"You don't own me," she cried, infuriated by his calm sureness.

"Oh, go to bed before you set fire to my temper again," he growled at her.

"Gladly," she returned. She went out the door without even a good night, and then lay awake half the night worrying about it.

Her dreams were full of Blake that night. And when she woke to the rumble of thunder and the sound of raindrops, she had a vivid picture of herself lying in his big arms while his mouth burned on her bare skin. It was embarrassing enough to make her late for breakfast. She didn't think she could have looked at Blake without giving herself away.

But her worries were groundless. Blake had already left to go to the office when Kathryn came downstairs to find Vivian sitting by herself at the breakfast table.

"Good morning," Vivian said politely. Her delicate blond features were enhanced by her buttercup yellow blouse and skirt. She looked slim and ultra-chic. She eyed Kathryn's jeans and roll-neck white sweater with disgust. "You don't believe in fashion, do you?" she asked.

"In my own home, no," she replied, reaching for cream to add to her steaming cup of coffee as Mrs. Johnson hustled back and forth between the kitchen, adding to the already formidable breakfast dishes.

Vivian watched her add two teaspoons of sugar to her coffee. "Don't count calories either, do you?" She laughed.

"I don't need to," Kathryn said quietly, refusing to display her irritation. Where in the world were Maude and Phillip and Dick Leeds?

Vivian watched her raise the cup to her mouth, and her hawk eyes lit on the slightly raw lower lip, which was faintly throbbing this morning—a painful reminder of Blake's shocking intimacy.

The blonde's narrow eyes darted down to her plate as she nibbled at scrambled eggs. "You and Blake were downstairs together a long time last night," she said conversationally.

"We...had some things to discuss," Kathryn murmured, hating the memory of him that came back to haunt her with a vengeance. She was being forced to see Blake in a new, different way, and she wasn't at all sure that she wanted to. She was more afraid of him now than ever: a delicious, mushrooming fear that made her pulse race at just the thought of his mouth crushing hers. What would it have been like, she wondered reluctantly, if he hadn't been angry...

"You missed Blake this morning," Vivian remarked, her eyes strangely wary as she watched Kathryn spoon eggs and ham onto her plate. "He asked me particularly to come down straightaway when the alarm went off so that we could have breakfast together."

"How nice," came the stilted reply.

Kathryn's head was bent, and she missed the faintly malicious smile that curled Vivian's full lips.

"He was anxious to leave before you came down," the blonde went on in a low, very cool voice. "I think he was afraid you might have read something more than he intended into what happened last night."

Kathryn's fork fumbled through her fingers and hit the china plate with a loud ringing sound. Her startled eyes jerked up. "W-what?" she faltered. "He *told* you?" she asked incredulously.

Vivian looked the picture of sophistication. "Of course, darling," she replied. "He was bristling with regrets, and I just let him talk. It was the dress, of course. Blake is too much a man not to be swayed by a half-naked woman."

"I was not...!"

"He makes love very well, don't you think?" Vivian asked with a secretive smile. "He's such a vibrant lover, so considerate and exciting..."

Kathryn's face was the color of red cabbage. She sipped her coffee, ignoring the blistering touch of it.

"You do understand that it mustn't be allowed to happen again?" the older woman asked softly, smiling at Kathryn coolly over her china cup. "I quite realize why Blake hasn't told you the true reason I came over here with my father, but..." she let her voice trail away insinuatingly.

Kathryn stared at her, feeling her secure, safe little world dissolving around her. It was like being buried alive. She could hardly breathe for the sudden sense of suffocation. "You mean...?"

"If Blake hasn't told you, I can't," Vivian said confidingly. "He didn't want to make the announcement straight away, you know. Not until his family had a chance to get to know me."

Kathryn couldn't manage words. So that was how it was. Blake planned to marry at last, and this blond barracuda was going to swim off with him. And after last night, she'd actually thought... Her face shuttered. What did it matter, anyway? Blake had always been like a brother, despite his brutal ardor last night. And that had only been to warn her, he'd said so. He was afraid she'd read something into it, was he? She'd show him!

Vivian, seeing the look of despair that came into the young girl's face, hid a smile in her coffee cup as she drained it. "I see you understand," she remarked smugly. "You won't let Blake know that I said anything?" she asked with a worried look. "He'd be so unhappy with me..."

"No, of course not," Kathryn said quietly. "Congratulations."

Vivian smiled sweetly. "I hope we're going to become great friends. And you mustn't think anything about what happened with Blake. He only wants to forget it, as you must. It was just a moment out of time, after all, nothing to be concerned about."

Of course not, Kathryn thought, feeling suddenly empty. She managed a bright smile, but fortunately the rest of the family chose that moment to join the two women, and she was able to bury her grief in conversation.

Kathryn had always liked the airport; it excited her to see the travelers with their bags and bright smiles, and she liked to sit and watch and speculate about them. A long-legged young woman, tall and tanned and blond, ran into the arms of a big, dark man and burst into tears. Studying them as she waited for Lawrence Donavan's plane to get in, Kathryn wondered if they were patching up a lovers' quarrel. They must have been, because the man was kissing her as if he never expected to see her again, and tears were running unchecked down her pale cheeks. The emotion in that hungry kiss made her feel like a peeping Tom, and she looked away. The depth of passion she sensed in them was as alien to her as the Andes. She'd never felt that kind of hunger for a man. The closest to it that she could remember coming was when Blake had kissed her the second time—that sensuous, aching touch that kindled fledgling responses in her untried body. If he'd kissed her a third time . . .

A movement caught her eye and she rose from the chair to find Larry Donavan coming toward her. She ran into his outstretched arms and hugged him, lifting her face for a firm, affectionate kiss.

His blue eyes laughed down into hers under the shock of red hair that fell rakishly across his brow.

"Miss me?" he teased.

She nodded, and the admission was genuine. "Would I fight half my family to drive this distance to pick you up if I hadn't?" she asked.

"I know. It is a pretty long drive, isn't it? I could have caught a bus . . ."

"Don't be silly," she said, linking her hand with his as they walked toward the baggage conveyor. "How would you like a grand tour of Charleston before we head home? Blake's guests got it, and you're just as entitled . . ."

"Guests?" he echoed. "Have I come at an inopportune time?" he asked quickly.

"Blake's courting a labor union and a woman at the same time," she said with a trace of bitterness in her tone. "We'll simply keep out of the way. Phillip and Maude and I will take care of you, don't worry."

"Blake's the guardian, isn't he?" he asked, pausing to grab his bag from the conveyor as it moved past.

"That, and a distant cousin. The Hamiltons raised me," she murmured. "I'm afraid it isn't the best weather for a visit," she apologized, gesturing toward the rainy gray skies as they stepped outside and walked toward the parking lot. "It's been raining off and on all day and we're expecting some flooding before we're through. Hurricanes really get to us in the low country."

"How low is it?" he asked.

She leaned toward him, taking the cue. "It's so low that you have to look up to see the streets."

"Same old Kat," he teased, using his own nickname for her, and he hugged her close. "It's good to be down south again."

"You only say that because you're glad to get away from all that pollution," she told him.

He blinked at her. "Pollution? In Maine?" he asked incredulously.

She batted her eyelashes up at him. "Why, don't you all have smokestacks and chemical waste dumps and bodies floating in the river from gang wars?" she asked in her best drawl.

He laughed brightly. "Stereotypes?"

She grinned. "Didn't you believe that we wore white bedsheets to the grocery store and drank mint juleps for breakfast when you first met me?"

"I'd never known anyone from the south before," he defended himself as they walked toward her small foreign car. "In fact," he admitted, "this really is the first time I've spent any time here."

"You'll learn a lot," she told him. "For instance, that a lot of us believe in equality, that most of us can actually read and write, and that..."

The sky chose that particular moment to open up, and rain started pouring down on them in sheets. She fumbled with her keys, barely getting them into the car in time to avoid a soaking.

Brushing her damp hair back from her face, Kathryn put the small white Porsche into reverse and backed carefully out of the parking space. It wasn't only due to her drivers' training course that she was careful at the wheel. When Blake had given her this car for her birthday last year, he'd been a constant passenger for the first week, watching every move she made. When he talked she listened, too, because in his younger days, Blake had raced in Grand Prix competitions all over Europe.

She swung into gear and headed out of the parking lot onto the busy street.

"It's raining cats!" She laughed, peering through the windshield wipers as the rain shattered against the metal roof with deafening force. It was hard to see the other cars, despite their lights.

"Don't blame me." Larry laughed. "I didn't bring it with me."

"I hope it lets up," she said uneasily, remembering the two bridges they had to cross to get back to King's Fort and on to Greyoaks. When flash floods came, the bridges sometimes were underwater and impossible to cross.

She saw an opening and pulled smoothly out into it.

"I see palm trees!" Larry exclaimed.

"Where did you think you were—Antarctica?" she teased, darting a glance at him. "They don't call us the Palmetto State for nothing. We have beaches in the low country, too, just like Florida."

He looked confused. "Low country?"

"The coastal plain is called that because . . . well, because it's low," she said finally. "Then there's the up country—but you won't see any of it this trip. King's Fort, where the family lives, is low country, too, even though it's an hour and a half away." She smiled apologetically. "I'm sorry we couldn't fly down to pick you up, but the big Cessna's having some part or other replaced. That's why Blake had to drive down for his guests. There's a company executive jet, too, but one of the vice-presidents had to fly down to another of the mills in Georgia."

He studied her profile. "Your family must own a lot of industries."

She shrugged. "Just three or four yarn mills and about five clothing manufacturing companies."

He lifted his eyes skyward. "Just, she says."

"Well, lots of Blake's friends own more," she explained. She headed straight down I-26 until she could exit and get onto Rutledge Avenue. "We'll go the long way around to the Battery, and I'll show you some of the landmarks on Meeting Street—if you can see them through the rain," she said drily.

"You know the city pretty well?" he asked, all eyes as they drove down the busy highway.

"I used to have an aunt here, and I stayed with her in the summer. I still like to drive down on weekends, for the night life."

She didn't mention that she'd never done it alone before, or that she was making this trip without Blake's knowledge or permission. Maude and Phillip had protested but nobody had ever stopped Kathryn except Blake, and they couldn't find him before she left. She could still see Vivian Leeds' smug expression, and her pride felt wounded. If he was involved with the blonde, he should never have touched Kathryn . . . but, then, she'd provoked him.

He'd accused her of it, and she couldn't deny it. All she didn't know was why.

"I'd like to use this as a location for a book," he said after they reached the turnoff onto the Battery, with its stone sea wall, and drove along it to Old Charleston.

She smiled at his excited interest as he looked first out at the bay and then across her at the rows of stately old houses.

They passed the Lenwood Boulevard intersection and he peered through the slackening rain. "Do you know any of the history of these old houses?" he asked.

"Some of them. Just a second." They drove on down South Battery Street and she pointed to a white two-story antebellum house on the right with long, elegant porches. "That one dates back to the 1820's. It was built on palmetto logs sunk in mud in an anti-earthquake design later used by Frank Lloyd Wright. It was one of only a few homes to survive the 1886 Charleston earthquake that destroyed most of the city."

"How about that!" He laughed, gazing back toward the house enclosed by its neat white picket fence.

She gestured toward White Point Garden where a small group of people were just disembarking from a horse-drawn carriage. "There are several carriage tours of the old part of town," she told him. "They're fun. I'm just sorry we don't have time today, but, then, it's not really the weather for it, either."

He sighed. "There wasn't a cloud in the sky when I left home."

"That's life," she told him. "Look on the left over there," she added when traffic let her turn onto Meeting Street. "That first house was once owned by one of the Middletons who owned Middleton Place Gardens. The second house is built in the Charleston 'double house' style—brick under cypress weather-boarding. It's late eighteenth century."

"Lady, you know your architecture," he said with grudging praise.

She laughed, relaxing in the plush leather seat. "Not like Aunt Hattie did. She taught me. A little farther down, there's a good example of the Adams-style construction—the Russell House. It's now the headquarters of the Historic Charleston Foundation."

He watched for it, and she caught a glimpse of smiling appreciation in his eyes as they studied the three-story building through its brick and wrought-iron wall.

"I wish we had time to go through Market Street," she said regretfully as she gave her attention to traffic. "There's a place where you can get every kind of food at individual stalls, and there are all kinds of shops and little art galleries . . ." She sighed. "But I guess we'd better stop at a restaurant a little closer to home. The wind's getting up, and I don't think the rain's any closer to quitting."

"Maybe on the trip back," he said with a smile, and winked at her.

She smiled back, flicking the radio on to a local station. The music blared for a few seconds, and then the weather report came on. She listened with a face that grew more solemn by the minute. Flash flood warnings were being announced for the area around King's Fort as well as the rivers near Charleston.

"I hope you're not hungry," she murmured as she turned back into Rutledge Avenue. "We've got to get home, before that flooding covers the bridges."

"Sounds adventurous," he chuckled, watching her intense concentration as she merged into traffic.

"It is. Are you hungry?" she persisted gently.

"I was rather thinking along the lines of a chilled prawn cocktail," he admitted with a grin.

"I'll have Mrs. Johnson fix you one when we get home," she promised. "We keep it, fresh-frozen, because it's Blake's favorite dish."

He stared out the window at the gray, darkening skies, lit by shop lights and car lights. "Some of those trees are bending pretty low," he remarked.

"I've seen them bend almost to the ground during a hurricane," she recalled nervously. "That's what this is about to be, I'm afraid. If I thought I could spare the time, I'd stop and call home. But I'm not going to risk it."

"You're the driver, honey," he said.

She smiled wryly. If Blake had been with her, he'd be at the wheel now, whether or not it was his car, taking over. She shifted in the seat. Comparisons were unfair, and she had no right to even be thinking about Blake now that he was practically engaged. But she couldn't help wondering what was going to happen when she got home. As Phillip had once said, Blake didn't particularly care how many people happened to be around if he lost his temper.

The rain followed them all the way to King's Fort, and despite Larry's periodic reassurances, Kathryn couldn't help worrying. The little sports car, in spite of its brilliant engineering and design, was too light for some of the deep puddles of water they soared through. Once, Kathryn almost went into a mailbox as the car hydroplaned over the center line. She recovered it in time, but she was getting more nervous by the minute. There was no place to stop until they got to King's Fort, or she'd have given it up.

She gritted her teeth and drove on, refusing to let her passenger see how frightened she really was. If only Blake had been with her!

They were approaching the first river bridge now, and she leaned forward with anticipation, peering through the heavy rain as she tried to see if the bridge was still passable.

"How does it look?" he asked. "I think I can still see the road . . . I can!"

"Yes," she breathed, relieved. She geared down to get a better view of the rising water. It was already over the banks and only inches below the low bridge. A few more minutes . . . she concentrated on getting across and didn't think about it.

"Is it much farther to the next bridge?" he asked.

"About twenty miles or so," she said tightly. He didn't say anything, but she knew he was thinking the same thing she was—that those few minutes might mean the difference between getting across or not.

There was almost no traffic on the road now. They only met two vehicles, and one of them was the state police.

"I hate to mention this," Larry said quietly. "But what if we can't get across the second bridge?"

She licked her dry lips "We'll have to go back to King's Fort and spend the night in the hotel," she said, thinking ahead to Blake's fury when he caught up with her. "But the river shouldn't be that high yet," she said soothingly. "I think we can make it."

"Just in case," he asked with a speaking glance, "what kind of temper does your guardian have?"

She tightened her hands on the wheel without answering.

When they reached the long river bridge, her worst fears were confirmed. Two uniformed men were just putting up a roadblock.

She rolled down her window as one of them approached. He touched his hat respectfully. "Sorry, ma'am," he said quietly, "you'll have to detour back to King's Fort. The river's up over the bridge."

"But it's the only road into Greyoaks," she protested weakly, knowing no argument was going to open up the road.

The uniformed man smiled apologetically. "The Hamilton estate? Yes, ma'am, I'm afraid it is. But there's no way across until the water level drops. I'm sorry."

She sighed. "Well, I'll have to go into King's Fort and call home . . ."

"You're out of luck there, too," the officer said with a rueful grin. "The telephone lines are down.

One way and another, it's been a rough day. I wish we could help.''

She smiled. "Thanks anyway."

She rolled the window back up and hesitated just a minute before she put the small car into reverse, turned it neatly around, and started back toward King's Fort.

"I feel bad about this," Larry said gently.

"Oh, don't be silly," she replied with a smile, "it's all right. We'll just be ... a little late getting home, that's all."

He studied her wan expression. "I'll explain it to him," he promised.

She nodded, but under her brave smile she felt like a naughty student on her way to the principal's office. Blake wasn't going to understand, and she sincerely hoped the river didn't go down until he cooled off.

Six

Kathryn pulled up in front of the King's Fort Inn and cut off the engine. She sat there for a minute with her hands tight on the wheel.

"Well, we tried," she said wryly, meeting Larry's sympathetic blue gaze. "I hope my insurance is paid up."

"Will he really be that mad?" he asked.

She drew in a hard breath. "I didn't have permission to come after you," she admitted. "I think I'm old enough to do without it. But Blake doesn't."

He patted her slender hand where it rested on the steering wheel. "I'll protect you," he promised, smiling.

She couldn't return the smile. The thought of Larry protecting her from Blake was almost comical.

The rain was still coming down as they ran into the hotel, and Kathryn held up her raincoat, making a tent over her wild, loosened hair. She laughed with exhilaration as they stopped under the awning to catch their breath.

He grinned down at her, his red hair unruly and beaded with rain. "Fancy meeting you here!"

"Not very fancy, I'm afraid." She laughed, putting a tentative hand up to her disorderly hair. "I must look like a witch."

He shook his head. "Lovely, as always."

"Thank you, kind sir." She darted a quick look at the hotel entrance. "It's the only hotel in town," she sighed, "and I'm sure we're going to cause some comment, but just ignore the stares and go ahead. We'll pretend we don't see any familiar faces."

"This town isn't all that small, surely," he remarked.

She smiled uncomfortably. "It's not. But, you see, the headquarters of the textile conglomerate is located here, and the family is fairly well known."

"I should have realized. Sorry."

"No need. Let's go in, shall we? You can get your bag later."

He followed her into the carpeted lobby. "What will you do for a change of clothes?" he asked.

She shrugged. "Do without, I suppose. Maybe in the..." Her voice trailed off, and she paled visibly.

Larry looked at her with a puzzled frown. She was staring at a big, dark man who was sitting in an armchair by the window reading a paper. He seemed vaguely weary, as if he'd been in that particular chair a long time. Even at a distance he looked threatening. As Larry watched, he deliberately put down the paper and got to his feet, to saunter over toward them.

Larry knew without being told who the man was. Kathryn's young face was stiff with apprehension. "Blake, I presume?" he murmured under his breath.

Kathryn's fingers dug into her slacks, making indentations in the soft beige fabric. She couldn't get the words out.

Blake rammed his big hands into his pockets, towering over her, his face expressionless. "Ready to go home?" he asked curtly.

"How... did you find me?" she whispered.

His dark eyes swept over her face. "I could find you in New York City at rush hour," he said quietly. Those fierce eyes shot across to Larry's face, and the younger man fought the urge to back away. He thought he'd met every kind of personality in the book, but this man was something beyond his experience. Authority clung to him like the brown slacks that hugged his muscular thighs, like the red knit shirt that emphasized the powerful muscles of his chest and arms.

"Donavan, isn't it?" Blake asked in a cutting tone.

"Y-yes, sir." Larry felt like a boy again. There was something intimidating about Blake Hamilton, and he knew without being told that he hadn't made the best of first impressions.

"The bridge is underwater," Kathryn said softly.

"I know." He started toward the exit, leaving them to follow.

"What about my poor car?" Kathryn persisted.

"Lock it and leave it," he threw over his shoulder. "We'll send back for it when the river goes down."

Kathryn looked at Larry helplessly. He nodded, and left them in front of the hotel under the awning. "I'll get my suitcase out, and lock the car for you," he told her.

She stood beside Blake, miserable and shivering from the chill of the rain.

"Why?" he asked, the single blunt word making her want to cry.

She sucked in a steadying breath. "It was only a short drive."

"With hurricane warnings out," he growled, looking down at her with barely contained fury behind his half-closed eyelids.

She drew her eyes away. "How are we going to get home?" she asked weakly.

"I ought to let you and your boyfriend walk," he replied coldly, staring out at the traffic in the wet street.

She looked down at her wet canvas shoes and then back up at him. He was only wearing a lightweight jacket with his shirt and trousers, and no raincoat.

"Don't you have an umbrella?" she asked gently.

He shifted his big shoulders, still not looking at her. "I didn't take time to look for it." His eyes glittered down at her, and his face hardened. "Have you any idea how long I've been sitting here wondering where you were?" he asked harshly.

She reached out and tentatively touched his sleeve. "I'm sorry, Blake, really I am. I wanted to call, but I was afraid to take the time..."

She suddenly noticed the new lines in his face, the bloodshot eyes. "Were you really worried?" she asked.

One big hand came out and ruffled her hair with rough affection. "What do you think?" he asked. Something in his face seemed to relax as he looked down into her soft eyes. "I've been out of my mind, Kate," he whispered, with such emotion in his voice that her heart seemed to lift up and fly.

"Blake..."

"Here I am!" Larry said merrily, joining them with his suitcase in his hand. "All locked up."

Kathryn folded her arms across her chest and tried to look calm. "How are we going to get across the river?" she asked Blake.

"I chartered a helicopter," he said with a wry smile.

She smiled. Leave it to Blake to make the most insurmountable problem simple.

Maude and Phillip had shared Blake's apprehension about the bad weather and Kathryn's absence, but they played it down. Vivian only shrugged when Kathryn told them about the rough trip home. She was much more interested in meeting another man to bat her false eyelashes at, Kathryn thought maliciously. The blonde was still glued to Blake and, remembering what was going on between them, Kathryn felt a twinge of pain. Blake had been worried about her, of course he had. But as his ward. Nothing more.

"You're very quiet tonight, darling," Phillip remarked when the rest of the family was gathered in the music room to hear Vivian play the grand piano. Kathryn had to admit that she was good. Larry, who played a little himself, sat and watched her with a rapt expression. It had all been a bit much for Kathryn, after the rough afternoon. She had slipped out into the hall and gone into the deserted kitchen to pour herself a cup of coffee. Phillip had followed her.

Sitting, her slender hands contracted around the cup, she crossed her legs, making her beige silk dress swish with the motion.

"I like that dress," Phillip remarked, perching himself on the edge of the table facing her. "One of the new ones, isn't it?"

She smiled and nodded. "Larry liked it, too."

"I like Larry," he grinned. "He makes me feel mature and venerable."

Her eyebrows flew up. "He what?"

"He's young, isn't he?" he asked drily, eyeing her over his cup.

"Ouch," she murmured impishly.

He laughed at her. "You know what I mean, don't you? Beside him, Blake looks even more formidable than usual." The grin faded. "Did he cut you up?"

"Blake?" She shook her head. "Surprisingly, no. I guess I should have told him I was going in the first place."

"Maude finally reached him in Atlanta." He emptied his cup and let it dangle in his hands. "He flew to Charleston, you know. It was a devil of a risk, but he took the chance. You were headed home by then. He had the state troopers after you."

Her face went pale. "I didn't realize...!"

"He'd been waiting three-quarters of an hour at the hotel when you got there," he added. "Sweating out every minute—along with the rest of us. Small cars are dangerous when it floods. I'm surprised he didn't really blow up. I imagine he felt like it."

She studied the coffee in her cup. "Yes, I imagine so," she whispered. Her eyes closed. She'd never have done it anyway if she hadn't been upset by what Vivian had told her at the breakfast table, but she couldn't tell Phillip about that. "It was a stupid thing to do."

"Just foolhardy," he corrected. "When are you going to stop fighting Blake?"

"When he lets go of me," she said curtly.

He only shook his head. "That could be a very long time..."

Greyoaks was imposing in the morning sunlight, and Kathryn reined up beside Larry to admire it.

She sighed. "You should see it in the spring when all the flowers are in bloom."

"I can imagine." His eyes swept over her slender body in her riding clothes. "You look completely at home on a horse."

She patted the Arabian mare's black mane. Sundance had been a little sluggish this morning, so she'd brought the mare instead. "I've been riding for a long time. Blake taught me," she added, laughing at the memories. "It was grueling, for both of us."

Larry sighed, studying the reins in his pale hands. "He doesn't like me."

"Blake?" She avoided his eyes. "He's hard to get close to," she said, knowing full well that wasn't completely true.

"If I planned to be here longer than three days," he admitted, "I think I'd buy a suit of armor. He makes me feel like an idiot."

"He's in the middle of labor disputes," she told him soothingly. "He and Dick Leeds are trying to work out some kind of agreement."

Larry smiled. "It looks like he's putting more effort into working on the daughter. A dish, isn't she? And talented, too."

Kathryn forced a smile onto her full lips. "Yes, she is."

"Are they engaged?" he asked with a sly glance. "I get a strong feeling that something's happening there."

"I think they are," she replied. "Let's head back, Larry. Mrs. Johnson hates to serve breakfast twice." She wheeled the mare and shot off ahead of him.

The question brought it all back. Of course they were engaged, and she couldn't understand why Blake was so concerned about keeping it a secret. The whole business made her angry. And Blake had told Vivian about... Her face flamed. She could never forgive him for that. And the conceit of the man, thinking that she was naive enough to read anything into that kiss. She'd put his treachery out of her mind yesterday, in the face of Blake's obvious concern for her safety. But now, with the danger over, it was burning holes in her temper. Damn Blake, anyway!

What you need, Kathryn Mary, she told herself as she leaned over the mare's black mane and gave her her head, is a place of your own!

She dismounted at the barn and waited for Larry to walk up to the house with her.

Blake and Vivian were the only ones at the breakfast table. Kathryn, smiling like a film star on display, clung to Larry's thin arm as they joined the others at the table.

"What a lovely ride," Kathryn sighed. She glanced at Vivian. "Do you like horses?" she asked.

"Can't stand them," Vivian said with a smile at Blake's taciturn face.

Kathryn's green eyes flashed, but she held onto her temper.

"The estate is very impressive," Larry remarked as he helped himself to bacon and eggs from the generous platters. "How many gardeners does it take to keep the grounds so neat?"

"Oh, Blake has three yard men, don't you, darling?" Vivian answered for him, leaning her muslin-clad shoulder briefly against his.

Kathryn wanted to sling scrambled eggs at her. She quickly lowered her eyes before any of her companions could read them.

"My parents have a garden about a fourth the size of yours," Larry continued, "without the gazebo. Dad's hobby is roses."

Blake lit a cigarette and leaned back in his chair to study the younger man with an unnerving intensity. "Do you grow flowers too?" he asked cuttingly.

"Blake!" Kathryn protested.

He didn't even glance at her. His whole attention was concentrated on Larry, who reddened and looked as if he might explode any minute. Despite his easygoing nature, he did have a temper, and it looked as if Blake was trying his best to make him lose it.

"Do you?" Blake persisted.

Larry put his cup down carefully. "I write books, Mr. Hamilton," he said tightly.

"What about?" came the lightning reply.

"Pompous asses, mostly," Larry grated.

Blake's dark eyes glittered dangerously. "Are you insinuating something, Donavan?"

"If the shoe fits . . ." Larry returned, his blue eyes icy.

"Stop it!" Kathryn burst out. She stood up, throwing her napkin onto the table. Her lower lip trembled, her eyes flashed. "Stop it, Blake!" she whispered furiously. "You've done nothing but pick on Larry since he got here! Do you have to . . . !"

"Be quiet," he said coldly.

She closed her lips as if he'd slapped her. "You're horrible, Blake," she whispered shakily. "Larry's a guest . . ."

"Not mine," he replied, glaring at Larry, who was standing now, too.

"You're right there," Larry replied gruffly. He turned to Kathryn. "Come and talk to me while I pack."

He left the room and Kathryn turned back at the doorway to glare at Blake. "If he leaves, I'll go with him, Blake," she told him furiously.

"You may think you will," he said in a soft, dangerous tone.

"We'll see about that," she choked, whirling.

Kathryn's pleas didn't deter Larry. He packed in record time and had started to call a cab when Dick Leeds came out into the hall and stopped him.

"Vivian wants to do some shopping in Charleston," he said with a quiet smile, "and since the river's down, it's quite safe. Phillip's going to drive us, and you're welcome to ride along. We'd be happy to drop you at the airport."

"Thank you," Larry said. He reached down and pecked Kathryn lightly on the cheek. "Sorry, love. I'm very fond of you, but not fond enough to take on your guardian."

She stiffened. "I'm sorry it worked out like this. Give my best to Missy."

He nodded. "Goodbye."

She watched him walk away with a sense of loss. It had all happened so fast. Her head was still spinning with the suddenness of it. She tried to piece together Blake's unreasonable behavior. He'd done his best to break up her friendship with Larry from the beginning. But why? He had Vivian. Why did he begrudge Kathryn a boyfriend? She hated him. Some-how, she had to get out from under his thumb....

She stayed out of sight until they left. Blake wasn't to be found, and she thought he'd gone with the rest. Maude had tried to persuade her to come along, to Vivian's obvious irritation, but she'd refused. She couldn't have borne being shut up in the same car with Larry and Blake both.

She walked through the damp hedges to the ga-zebo. The grass and shrubs were still wet from the previous day's heavy rains, but inside the quiet con-fines of the little white building with its delicate lat-ticework and ring of cushions, it was dry and cozy.

She sat down on the plush cushions and looked out over the cobblestone walks that led around and through the well-kept gardens. Although the azaleas and dogwoods that bloomed gloriously in the spring were not in season now, the roses gave the gardens a dash of color. The fragrance of the white ones was delicious. She closed her eyes and drank it in, along with the warm breeze that made the September day more like summer.

"Sulking?"

She jumped at the sound of Blake's deep, curt voice. Her startled eyes found him in the entrance of the small building, a smoking cigarette in his hand. He was wearing the same beige slacks and yellow knit shirt he'd had on at the breakfast table, and the same forbidding scowl.

She scowled back, curling her jodhpur-clad leg under her slender body, tugging her white sweater down. "Haven't you done enough for one morning?" she asked angrily.

One dark eyebrow went up. "What have I done? I didn't ask him to leave."

"No," she agreed hotly. "You just made it impossible for him to stay and hold on to his pride."

He shrugged indifferently. "In any case, it's no great loss."

"To you," she added. "Your girlfriend's still here."

He eyed her carefully. "Yes," he said. "She is."

"Naturally. She's *your* guest."

He shouldered away from the entrance and walked toward her, stopping just in front of her. "Would you really want a man who was afraid of me?"

Her eyes shot up to his. "No," she admitted sharply. "I'd like one who'd beat the devil out of you."

A slow, mischievous smile touched his mouth. "Had any luck yet?"

She tore her gaze away, remembering Jack Harris and a string of others. "Why didn't you go with them? Vivian seemed to have taken a shine to Larry last night."

"Vivian's tastes are not necessarily mine."

Kathryn stared down at the dark green cushions, tracing a pattern on the one where she was sitting with a nervous finger.

"Why wouldn't you let him stay, Blake?" she asked bitterly. "He wasn't bothering you."

"He wasn't?" He finished the cigarette and flung it out on the cobblestones, where it lay smouldering briefly until the dampness doused it. "The damned young fool, letting you drive in that downpour! I should have broken both his legs!"

She gaped at him. "It was my car, he couldn't very well tell me to let him get behind the wheel!"

"I could," he replied gruffly. "And I would have. If I'd been with you, you'd never have left Charleston."

She couldn't repress a tiny smile: It was exactly what she'd been thinking on the way home. "There was a moment or two there when I wish you had been," she said lightly.

He didn't reply, and when she looked up, it was to find his face strangely rigid.

"You shouldn't have worried," she added, aware of a new tension between them. "You taught me to drive, remember?"

"All I remembered was that you were in danger in the company of a fool, a boy who didn't know how to take care of you," he said tightly. "If anything had happened to you, I'd have killed him."

He didn't raise his voice. But the words had as much impact as if he'd shouted them.

"What a violent thing to say," she laughed nervously.

He didn't smile. His dark eyes narrowed, spearing her with an intensity that made flames kindle in her blood. "I've always been violent about you. Are you just now noticing it?"

She gazed up at him quietly, stunned by the words, by the emotion in them, her lips slightly parted, her eyes curious and soft.

Blake leaned one big hand on the back of the seat over her shoulder and his eyes dropped to her soft mouth. The action had brought him closer; so close that she could smell the clean, masculine fragrance of soap and cologne, feel the warmth of his big body.

"Blake," she whispered, yielding without words, without thought, longing for him.

He bent his dark head and brushed his mouth against hers, a whisper of delicious sensation that quickened her pulse, her breathing. He drew back, and she lifted a finger to trace, tremulously, the hard, sensuous curve of his mouth. Emotion trembled between them in the silence, broken only by the whispering breeze, and the distant sound of a songbird.

His lips moved, catching her exploring finger, and she felt the tip of his tongue moving softly against it. Her eyes looked straight into his, and she read the excitement in them.

He searched her flushed young face quietly. "Stand up, Kathryn," he said at last. "I want to feel you against me."

Like a sleepwalker, she obeyed him, letting him draw her so close that she could feel his powerful thighs pressing against hers, the muscles of his chest like a wall against her soft breasts.

His thumb brushed against her mouth and he studied it as if he needed to memorize it. "Are you afraid?" he asked in a strange, husky voice.

She shook her head, meeting his eyes with the hunger and need plain in her own. "Last time..."

"It's not going to be like last time," he breathed. "Kate...!" Her soft mouth parted eagerly as his lips met hers.

Her slender arms reached up around his neck, holding him, and she kissed him back feverishly, trying to show that she could be anything he wanted her to be.

His big hand tangled in the thick strands of hair at her nape, and his devouring mouth forced hers open even wider. He explored it with a deepening intimacy that made her tremble. With a sense of wonder she felt his hands at her back, sliding under the sweater and up to move caressingly against her silken skin.

"No bra?" he murmured against her mouth, and she could feel the amused smile that moved his lips.

She flushed at the intimacy of the question, and suddenly reached around to catch his wrists and hold them as he started to slide his exploring hands around under her arms.

"Blake . . ." she protested.

He chuckled softly and drew his hands away, to replace them at her waist over the thick fabric. "You said you weren't afraid," he reminded her.

She lowered her eyes to his broad chest. "Must you make fun of me?" she asked miserably. "You know I'm not sophisticated."

"It's quite obvious," he laughed softly. "If you were, you would know better than to plaster yourself against a man when he kisses you. Ten years ago, I'm not sure I'd have been able to draw back."

She looked up, startled. "But in the movies . . ."

"Plastic people, contrived situations; this is real, Kathryn." He took her hand and pressed it inside the opening of his shirt, against the hard, warm flesh and thick mat of hair. She felt the heavy rhythm of his heart. "Do you feel it?" he asked softly. "You make my blood run like a river in flood, Kate."

She was lost in his dark eyes, in the gentleness of his deep voice. Her fingers lingered inside his shirt, liking the feel of his muscular body, remembering suddenly and vividly the way he looked that night long ago with Jessica.

He seemed to read the thoughts in her mind. Abruptly he caught her hands and slid them under the shirt to lie against the broad, hard chest. Her fingers trembled on the hair-rough skin.

"I've never touched . . . anyone like this," she whispered, awed by the new longings surging through her body, making her tremble in his big arms. "I never wanted to, until now."

His lips brushed against her forehead, his breath warm and a little unsteady, while her curious fingers explored the powerful muscles.

She raised her eyes to Blake's. "I . . . Blake, I feel . . ."

His fingers pressed gently against her lips. "Kiss me," he whispered. "Don't think, don't talk. Just kiss me." His lips teased hers delicately, softly, causing a surge of hunger that dragged a moan from her tight throat.

She went on tiptoe to help him, to tempt him, her lips parting under the lazy pressure of his mouth as he began to deepen the kiss. She felt his hands caressing her back, moving surely around to her ribcage. But, this time, she didn't catch his wrists.

His thumbs edged out to trace the gentle slope of her high, firm breasts and she stiffened instinctively at the unfamiliar touch.

"It's all right," he whispered at her lips. "Don't pull away from me."

Her eyes opened, wide and curious and a little frightened. "It's... new," she whispered.

"Being touched?" he asked quietly. "Or being touched by me?"

"Both," she admitted.

His fingers moved higher, and he watched her face while they found the hard peaks and traced them tenderly, just before his hands swallowed the velvet softness and pressed against it with warm, sensuous motions.

"How does it feel, Kate?" he asked in a deep, honeyed tone. "Is it good?"

Her nails dug into his chest involuntarily as the magic worked on her, and she moaned softly.

"I shouldn't... let you," she whispered.

"No, you shouldn't," he agreed, moving closer. "Tell me to stop, Kate," he whispered. "Tell me you hate it."

"I...wish I could," she whispered. His mouth was on her closed eyelids, her nose, her high cheekbones, while his hands made wild shivers of sensation wash over her bare skin.

His mouth bit at hers tenderly in a succession of teasing kisses that made her want to cry out. "God, you're sweet," he whispered huskily. "As soft as a whisper where I touch you."

Her fingers tangled in the mat of hair over his strong chest. "I . . . dreamed about how it would be with you," she whispered shakily. "Ever since that night I saw you with Jessica, I've wondered . . ."

"I know," he whispered back, "I saw it in your eyes. That was what wrung me out so, Kate, because I wondered, too. But you were so damned young . . ."

She drew a deep, unsteady breath, lifting her body higher against his deft, sure hands. "Blake . . . ?" she moaned.

"What do you want?" His dark eyes burned into hers. "There's nothing you can't ask me, don't you know that? What do you want, Kate?"

Her body ached with the newness of wanting and she didn't know how to put into words what she needed. It had never been like this, never!

"I don't know how to say it," she admitted in a breathless whisper. "Blake . . . please . . ."

He bent, lifting her in his big arms without a word, and carried her to the cushioned seat that ringed the gazebo. Then he came down beside her with something in his hard, dark face that was faintly shocking after all the years of banter and camaraderie and deep affection. She was just beginning to see Blake as a lover, and the effect it was having on her defied description. She looked up at him with all her confusion in her green eyes, and in her flushed, expectant face.

"I won't hurt you," he said softly.

"I know." She lifted her fingers to his hard, chiseled mouth and traced it gently. "I've never kissed a man lying down."

"Haven't you?" He smiled as he lifted himself to ease his formidable torso down onto her, so that they were thigh to thigh, hip to hip, breast to breast. She gasped at the intimate contact and her fingers dug into the rippling muscles of his shoulders.

His fingers cupped her face as he bent. "Am I too heavy, Kate?" he whispered against her soft mouth.

She flushed at the question, but she didn't look away. "No," she managed shakily.

He brushed his mouth across hers. "Pull your sweater up," he whispered.

"Blake..."

He kissed her closed eyelids. "You want it as much as I do," he breathed. "Pull it up, Kate . . . then help me pull up my shirt."

She looked into his eyes, trembling. She wanted him until she ached from head to toe, but he was suggesting an intimacy she'd never experienced before, and once it happened, there wouldn't be any going back.

"It's . . . I mean, I've never . . ." she stammered.

His thumbs brushed against the corners of her mouth while his tongue lightly traced the trembling line of her lips.

"Don't you want to feel me against you like that, Kate?" he whispered sensuously. "With nothing between us?"

She gasped against his invading mouth. Her eyes closed tightly. "Yes," she ground out, and even her voice trembled. "Oh, Blake, yes, yes . . . !"

"Help me," he whispered huskily.

With trembling fingers, she lifted the hem of his yellow knit shirt and eased it up over the warm, hard muscles under their mat of crisp black hair, and her fingers savored the sensuous contact with him, while her heart pounded out a mad rhythm.

His mouth coaxed hers open, tasting it, gentling it, his fingers tenderly caressing her face.

"Now yours, love," he whispered softly. "There's nothing to be afraid of, nothing at all, I won't hurt you, I won't force you. Now, Kate..."

She looked into his darkening eyes while she slid the soft sweater up over her taut breasts and with a shuddering pleasure, she felt him ease down again until her taut nipples vanished into the dark pelt over his chest. She felt his body against hers in a contact that made magic in her mind and she gasped.

"My God, isn't it delicious?" he whispered tautly, shifting his powerful torso slowly, sensuously, across her breasts in the utter silence of the gazebo.

Her fingers hesitated on his hard collarbone, lightly touching him, feeling him. Her eyes widened as the intimacy sent her pulse racing, as her breath caught in her throat.

"You're...so warm," she whispered.

"A man being burned alive does feel warm," he replied half-humorously. He moved then, holding her eyes while his body eased completely onto hers.

"It's all right," he breathed, calming her as she stiffened involuntarily at the greater intimacy with his body. His hands stroked her hair lightly, his forearms taking the bulk of his weight. He studied her closely. "Now I can feel you completely," he whispered, "and you can feel me. We can't hide anything from each other when we touch like this, can we, Kate? You know without words how much I want you, don't you?''

She flushed wildly as the exact meaning of his words got through to her, and she noticed for the first time all the differences between his body and hers.

Pleasure surged up in her like spring sap in a young tree as she sensed her own awakening to emotions and sensations that had lain dormant inside her, waiting for a catalyst.

Her fingers touched his face, his mouth, his arrogant nose, his thick dark brows, and when she breathed, she was made even more aware of the warmth and weight of his hair-roughened chest against the sensitive warmth of her bareness.

The weight of him crushed her yielding body down into the soft cushions and her arms went up to hold him even closer as he bent to take her mouth under his.

She opened her lips, her fingers tangling in his thick, cool hair as the kiss went on and on. His tongue darted into her mouth, demanding, tormenting, while his hands slid under her thighs and lifted her body up against his with a bruising pressure, until she was achingly aware of how much he wanted her.

She shifted restlessly under the crush of his body, and a hard groan tore out of his throat while he kissed her. A shudder ran the length of him.

"Don't do that," he whispered against her lips. "I may be past my first youth, but I can lose my head with you so easily it isn't even funny."

She watched him, fascinated. "I . . . I like the way it feels, to lie with you like this," she admitted in a whisper.

"My God, I like it, too," he groaned. "Kiss me, honey . . . !"

His hungry ardor flared like wildfire between them. She stopped trying to understand and melted into him. It was glorious, the hungry crush of his mouth, the feel of his arms, the long, hard contact with his powerful body, the warmth of him that seemed to burn her everywhere they touched. She never wanted this kiss to end. She wanted to spend the rest of her life in his arms like this, holding him, loving him. Loving him!

He caught her wrists abruptly and tore her clinging hands away from his back. He looked down at her as if he'd been temporarily out of his mind and had only just realized what he was doing. He shook his dark head as if to clear it. With a violent movement he got to his feet and pulled his shirt down, keeping his back to Kathryn while she fumbled, embarrassed, with her sweater. She stared at his broad back incredulously. She'd forgotten what had happened just an hour ago, forgotten the anger and frustration she'd felt. In the shadow of Blake's blazing ardor she'd even forgotten Vivian. How could she have let him . . . !

He turned, catching that expression of shock in her eyes, and something seemed to harden his face, take the soft light out of his eyes. He smiled mockingly.

"Now tell me you miss Donavan," he said in a voice that cut through her heart like a razor.

She licked at the inside of her swollen lips, tasting the lingering touch of his mouth there, her eyes vulnerable, hurt.

"Was that why?" she asked in a sore whisper getting to her feet.

He rammed his hands into his pockets. His face was harder than she could ever remember seeing it.

"Or was it . . . because you don't want another man to have me?" she asked painfully.

"I've got all the bodies I need, Kate," he said tightly "I didn't raise you to take you into my bed the minute you came of age."

"But, just now . . ." she began hesitantly.

"I want you, all right," he admitted, scowling down at her. "I have for a long time. But just because I lost my head with you a minute ago, that doesn't mean I plan to do anything about it.''

Of course not, how could he, when he planned to marry Vivian? "Don't worry," she said bitterly, stepping away from him. "I'm not going to 'read anything' into it this time either."

"What?"

"That's what you told Vivian, isn't it?" she asked in a broken voice, slanting a glance back at him as she stepped down into the garden. "That you were afraid I might 'read something' into what happened the other night? I'm not a child, Blake, I quite realize that men can be attracted physically by women they don't even like, much less love."

"Just what are you talking about?" he demanded, his eyes blazing.

"Vivian told me yesterday how much you regretted your actions the other night!" she threw at him.

The expression on his hard face puzzled her, if a fleeting shadow could be called that. "She told you that?" he asked.

She whirled. "No, I just made it up for the fun of it!"

"Kate . . . !"

"Don't call me Kate!" She glared back at him through her tears, missing the sudden glint in his dark eyes. "I hate you. And I'm going to get a job and my own apartment, and you can drag Vivian off into gazebos and make love to her! I don't ever want you to touch me again, Blake!''

"You will," he said in a strange, deep tone.

She turned and ran back toward the house as if invisible phantoms were chasing after her. She locked her bedroom door behind her and threw herself down onto the bed, venting the stored-up tears. She loved Blake. Not as she always had, as a protector, but newly, differently, as a man. She could barely believe it had happened, and she didn't want to admit it even in the privacy of her own mind. She loved Blake. And he was going to marry Vivian. Her eyes closed in pain. Vivian, living here, loving Blake, too, touching him, kissing that hard, beautiful mouth...

She groaned out loud with anguish. She'd have to get a job. There was no way around it now. She sat up, drying her tears. She'd start looking first thing in the morning, Blake or no Blake, and find something that she could do to make a living for herself. There was no way she could go on living under the same roof with Blake and his wife!

Seven

She was purposely late for breakfast, and when she got downstairs she glanced around quickly, hoping to find that Blake had already eaten.

Maude was just finishing a piece of toast across from Phillip, who was sipping his coffee. Blake, Dick Leeds and Vivian were nowhere in sight.

"My, aren't you dressed up," Maude commented, her approving glance resting on Kathryn's pretty beige suit and crepe de chine eggshell blouse with its neat bow. Her hair was drawn into a soft chignon, with wisping curls around her face, her feet encased in spike-heel open-toed sandals in beige and brown. She looked the picture of working woman-hood.

"Trendy-looking," Phillip added with a wink. "Where are you off to in your fine feathers, little bird?"

"I'm going to get a job," she said with a cool smile.

Maude choked on her toast and had to be thumped on the back by Phillip.

"A job?" she gasped. "Doing what, Kathryn?"

"It depends on what I can find," the younger woman said with a stubborn light in her green eyes. "Now, don't argue, Maude," she added, catching the quick disapproval in the pale, dark-eyed face.

"I wasn't going to, dear," Maude protested. "I was just going to ask how you planned to tell Blake."

"She already has," Blake told them, appearing in the doorway dressed in a becoming gray suit with a patterned tie that emphasized his darkness. "Let's go, Kate."

She sat there almost trembling with emotion, her wide green eyes pleading with him, even as she knew she wasn't going to fight. All her resolutions vanished when Blake confronted her. After yesterday, all the fight was gone, anyway. She didn't have the heart for it anymore.

"She hasn't had breakfast," Phillip observed.

"She'll learn to get downstairs in time, won't she?" Blake replied, and there was something vaguely menacing about the way he was looking at his younger brother.

Phillip grinned sheepishly. "Just an observation, big brother." He laughed.

Blake's dark eyes went to Kathryn, skimming over her possessively. "I said, let's go."

She got up, leaving a cup of fresh coffee and a plate of scrambled eggs behind her as she followed him out into the hall apprehensively.

"Where are we going?" she asked.

Both heavy brows went up. He opened the front door for her. "To work, of course."

"But, I don't have a job yet."

"Yes, you do."

"What as?" she asked.

"My secretary."

She followed him out to his dark sedan in a daze, only speaking when they were going down the driveway at Blake's usual fast pace.

"Did I hear you right?" she asked, and stared at his profile with unconcealed disbelief.

"You did." He took out his cigarette case and extracted a cigarette from it as he drove, leaning over to push in the cigarette lighter.

"But, Blake, I can't work for you," she protested.

His dark eyes scanned her face briefly. "Why not?"

"I can't type fast enough," she said, grasping at straws. Having to be near him all day, every day, would be more agony than ecstasy.

"You're about average, little one. You'll do." He lit his cigarette and pushed the lighter back in place. "You said you wanted a job," he reminded her.

She watched cars in the other lane passing by them, not really seeing anything as she sat stiffly beside Blake.

"Where was Vivian this morning?" she asked quietly. "The two of you were out late last night."

"So we were," he said noncommitally.

"It's none of my business, of course," she said tightly, avoiding his eyes.

He only smiled, keeping his attention on the road.

The Hamilton Mills complex was located in a sprawling ground level facility in the city's huge industrial park, modern and landscaped. Kathryn had been inside the building many times, but never as an employee.

She followed Blake into his attractive carpeted office, where the dark furniture was complemented by elegant furnishings done in chocolates and creams.

Her eye was caught and held by a portrait that spanned the length of the big leather sofa under it. She stared at the sweeping seascape, the sunset colors mingling in the clouds, the palm-lined beach a swath of white and silver. In the foreground were the shadowy outlines of a man and a woman.

"Like it?" he asked as he checked the messages on his desk.

She nodded. "It's St. Martin, isn't it?" she asked quietly. "I recognize that spot."

"You ought to. We shared a bottle of champagne under that spread of trees on your eighteenth birthday. I nearly had to carry you back to the beach house."

She laughed, remembering her own bubbling pleasure that night, Blake's company and the sound of the surf. They'd talked a lot, she recalled, and waded in the foaming surf, and drunk champagne, while Phillip and Maude visited one of the casinos and lost money.

"It was the best birthday party I ever had," she murmured. "I don't think we had a cross word the whole trip."

"Would you like to do it again?" he asked suddenly.

She turned. He was standing in front of his desk, his legs slightly apart, his hands on his lean hips.

"Now?" she asked.

"Next week. I've got some business in Haiti," he explained mysteriously. "I thought we might stay in St. Martin for a few days and I could go on to Haiti from there."

"Why Haiti?" she asked, curious.

"You don't have to come on that leg of the trip," he said with a finality that permitted no further questioning.

She studied the painting again. "We?" she asked in a bare shadow of her normal voice.

"Vivian and Dick, too," he admitted. "A last-ditch effort to get his cooperation."

"And hers?" she asked with more bitterness than she knew.

There was a long pause. "I thought you knew by now why she came along."

She dropped her eyes to the huge wood frame of the painting, feeling dead inside. So he was finally admitting it. "Yes," she whispered. "I know."

"Do you? I wonder," he murmured, scowling at her downcast face.

"Is anyone else coming?" she asked. "Phillip?"

"Phillip?" he said harshly. His face hardened "What's going on between you two, Kathryn Mary?"

"Nothing," she said defensively. "We just enjoy each other's company, that's all."

Blake's dark eyes seemed to explode in flames. "By all means, we'll take Phillip. You'll have to have someone to play with!" His voice cut.

"I'm not a child, Blake," she said with quiet dignity.

"You're both children."

She squared her slender shoulders. "You didn't treat me like one yesterday!"

A slow, faint smile touched his hard mouth. "You didn't act like one." His bold, slow eyes sketched her body in the becoming suit.

She felt the color creeping into her cheeks at the words, remembering the feel of his warm chest, the hair-roughened texture of it against her breasts.

"Phillip," he scoffed, catching her eyes and holding them. "You'd burn him alive. You're too passionate for him. For Donavan, too."

"Blake!" she burst out, embarrassed.

"Well, it's true," he growled, his eyes narrowing on her face, darkening with memory. "I barely slept last night. I could feel your hands touching me... Your body like silk, twisting against mine. You may be green, little girl, but you've got good instincts. When you finally stop running from passion, you'll be one hell of a woman."

"I'm not running..." she whispered involuntarily before she realized what she was saying.

She stood there watching him, suddenly vulnerable, hungry as she remembered the touch of his hands against her bare skin and the violence of his emotion. She wanted to touch him. To hold him. To feel his mouth against hers... He read that surge of longing accurately. His eyes darkened violently as he rose and came around the desk toward her. There was no pretense between them now; only a thread of shared hunger that was intense and demanding.

"You'd damned well better mean what I read in your eyes," he growled as he reached her, his big hands shooting out to catch her roughly by the waist and pull her close.

She gloried in the feel of his big, muscular body against the length of hers. Her face lifted to his and her heart floundered as her eyes met his from a distance of scant inches. His head started to bend, and she trembled.

His mouth was hungry, and it hurt. She reached up, clinging to him, while his lips parted hers and burrowed into them ardently.

"Blake," she whispered achingly.

His big hand moved up from her waist to cover her breast, taking its slight weight as his tongue shot into the warmth of her mouth.

"You're in my blood like slow poison, Kate," he whispered roughly. His fingers contracted, and he watched the helpless reaction on her flushed face. "I look at you, and all I can think about is how you feel under my hands. Do you remember how it was between us yesterday?" he whispered against her mouth. "Your breasts crushed against me and not a stitch of fabric to stop us from feeling each other's skin..."

"Oh, don't," she moaned helplessly. "It isn't fair..."

"Why isn't it?" he demanded. He lifted her until her eyes were on a level with his. "Tell me you didn't want what I did to you in the gazebo. Tell me you weren't aching every bit as much as I was when I let you go."

She couldn't, because she had wanted him, and it was in every line of her flushed face, in the wide green eyes that searched his helplessly in the silence of the office.

"I'd like to take you to Martinique alone, do you know that?" he breathed huskily. "Just the two of us, Kate, and I'd lay you down in the sand in the darkness and taste every soft, sweet inch of your body with my lips."

Her breath caught at the passionate intensity in the words. "I... I wouldn't..."

"Like hell you wouldn't," he whispered. His mouth took hers hungrily, his hands slid down to grasp her hips and grind them sensuously into his until she cried out at the sensations it caused.

"Want me, Kate?" he taunted in a deep whisper. "God knows, I want you almost beyond bearing. It was a mistake for me to touch you the way I did. Now all I can think about is how much more of you I want. Kiss me, honey. Kiss me..."

She did, because at that moment it was all she wanted from life. The feel of him, the touch and taste and smell of him, Blake's big arms riveting her to every inch of his powerful body while his mouth took everything hers had to give. It seemed like a long time later when he finally raised his head to let his eyes blaze down into hers.

With a suddenness that was almost painful, the door swung open and Vivian's high-pitched voice shattered the crystal thread of emotion binding them.

"Well, hello," she said in her clear British accent. "I do hope I'm not interrupting anything?"

"Of course not," Blake said, turning to her with magnificent composure and a smile. "I promised you a tour, didn't I? Let's go. Kate," he said over his shoulder, "You come along, too."

She was still trembling, and she longed to refuse. But Vivian's eyes were already suspicious, and she didn't dare.

Blake escorted them through the huge manufacturing company, pointing out the main areas of interest—the training room where the new seamstresses were taught how to use the latest modern equipment; the pants line, where each sewing machine operator performed a different function in the manufacture of a pair of slacks; the cutting room, where huge bales of cloth were spread on long tables and cut by men with jigsaws through multiple layers of thickness. Kathryn remembered the terms peculiar to the garment industry from her childhood: "bundle boys" who carried the bundles of pattern pieces out to the sewers; "foreladies" who were the overseers for each group of seamstresses; "spreaders" who spread the cloth; "cutters" who cut it; and "inspectors" who were responsible for catching second and third quality garments before they could be shipped out as "firsts." Then there were the pressers and packers and the "lab lady" who washed test garments. Hundreds of sewing machines were running together in the room where the shirt line was located, and this section had button-holing machines as well as the other equipment found on the pants line. Kathryn's eye was caught by the brilliant colors.

"That shade of blue is lovely!" she exclaimed.

Blake chuckled. "I'll have to take you through the yarn mill sometime and show you how it's made. Bales of cotton go through a process that takes a rope of raw material and runs it through a volley of spindles in different rooms to produce a thread of yarn. We use cotton and rayon now. In the old days, the mill ran strictly on cotton."

"How interesting," Vivian said with little enthusiasm. "I've never actually been in a mill."

Kathryn gaped at her. This wasn't *her* first trip by a long shot. She was forever tagging along after Blake and Phillip in her younger days, because the whole process of making clothing had fascinated her. But she hadn't been in a yarn mill since her childhood, and she'd been too young to understand much of what she'd seen then.

"How many blouses come out of here in a week?" Kathryn asked, watching blouses in different states of readiness at each machine row as they walked past. She had to practically yell in Blake's ear to make him hear her above the noise.

"About ten thousand dozen," he told her, smiling at her shocked expression. "We've added a lot of new equipment here. We have over six hundred sewing machine operators in this plant, and it takes about a hundred and fifty thousand yards of material a week to keep these women busy."

Kathryn looked back the way they'd come. "The slacks . . . ?"

"That's a separate plant, honey," he reminded her, glancing toward the door that linked the two divisions. "We only have about three hundred machines on the pants line. Our biggest business here is blouses."

"It's enormous!" she exclaimed.

Blake nodded. "We do a volume business. We have contracts with two of the biggest mail order houses, and you'll remember that we have our own chain of outlet stores across the country. It's a hell of a big operation."

"It must make lots of money," Vivian commented, and Kathryn saw dollar signs in the older woman's eyes.

Blake's eyebrow jerked, but he didn't reply.

When they finished the tour, Vivian persuaded Blake to take her out for coffee, and he left Kate with a dictaphone full of letters to be typed. It rankled her that Vivian, who had gotten her breakfast at home, was being treated to coffee and doughnuts while Kathryn, who had been dragged away from her breakfast, got nothing. She was somewhat mollified a half hour later when Blake came back and set coffee in a styrofoam cup and a packaged pastry in front of her on the desk.

"Breakfast," he said. "I seem to recall making you miss yours."

She smiled up at him, surprised and pleased, and her face lit up.

"Thanks, Blake," she said gently.

He shrugged his powerful shoulders and strode over to the dividing door between her office and his. "Any problems with the dictaphone?" he asked over his shoulder.

"Only with your language," she remarked, tongue-in-cheek.

He lifted an amused eyebrow at her. "Don't expect to reform me, Kate."

"Oh, I don't know a woman brave enough to try, Blake," she said with angelic sweetness to his retreating back. Switching off the electric typewriter, she opened her steaming coffee.

It was almost quitting time when Phillip stopped by the office to see Blake. He leaned his hands on Kathryn's desk and grinned at her.

"Slaving away, I see," he teased lightly.

She sighed. "You don't know the half of it," she groaned. "I never realized how much correspondence it takes to keep a plant like this one going.

Blake even writes to congressmen and state senators and the textile manufacturers association—by the way, I didn't realize he was president of it this year."

"See how much you're learning?" Phillip teased. He reached out a hand and tipped her chin up, bending close to whisper, "Has Blake flicked you with his whip yet?"

Her eyes opened wide and she smiled. "Does he have one?" she whispered back.

It was pure bad luck that Blake should choose that moment to open his office door. He glared at Phillip so blackly that the younger man backed away from the desk and actually reddened.

Blake jerked his office door shut. "Take Kathryn home with you," he told his brother curtly. "Vivian and I are going out to supper."

And he left the office without even a backward glance, while Kathryn sat there with her heart in her shoes, wondering how Blake could have been so loving earlier in the day and so hateful now. What had she done? Or was it just that Blake was already feeling regrets?

The days fell into a pattern. Kathryn rode to work with Blake every morning, and back with him in the evenings. Although he was business-as-usual in his dealings with her, Vivian seemed to purple when Kathryn and Blake left together. The blonde did everything except lobby for a job of her own to try to take up Blake's free time. And she succeeded very well.

By Saturday, Kathryn was ready for some relaxation, and since Vivian had talked Blake into taking her by plane for a shopping trip to Atlanta, Kathryn asked Phillip to go with her to one of the new malls in town. The request seemed to irritate Blake, but Kathryn ignored his evident displeasure. After all, what right did he have to interfere with her life? He was too wrapped up in Vivian to care what she did. Even the thought of going to the islands with him was frightening now—although she knew she'd never be strong enough to renege on her promise to accompany him. She loved him too much, wanted to be with him too much, to refuse. He might marry Vivian, but at least Kathryn would have a few memories to tuck away.

"You're walking me to death," Phillip groaned, hobbling with exaggeration to the nearest bench in the busy mall. He eased down with a stage sigh and smile.

"We've only been in five shops," she reminded him. "You can't possibly be tired."

"Five shops, where you tried on fifteen outfits each," he corrected.

She plopped down beside him, sighing wearily. "Well, I'm depressed," she said. "I had to do something to cheer me up."

"I'm not depressed," he said with a sigh. "Why did I have to come along?"

"To carry the packages," she said sensibly.

"But, Kathryn, love, you haven't bought anything."

"Yes, I have. In that little boutique we just came from."

His eyebrows lifted. "What?"

"This." She handed him a small sack containing a jeweler's box with a pair of dainty sapphire and diamond earrings inside. "Aren't they lovely? I charged them to Blake."

"Oh, no," he groaned, burying his face in his hands.

"Anyway, you can carry them," she said, "so you'll feel necessary."

"How will I ever survive all these honors you confer upon me?" he asked with mock humility.

"Don't be nasty," she chided, pushing against his shoulder with her own as they sat side by side. "I really am depressed, Phil."

He studied her dejected little face. "What's wrong, kitten? Want me to slay a dragon for you?"

"Would you?" she asked hopefully, her green eyes wide. "You could sneak up on her while she's sleeping, and..."

"Your eyes need checking," he remarked, lifting an eyebrow at her as he folded his arms and leaned back against the wooden bench. "Vivian isn't a dragon."

"That's what you think," she muttered. "Wait until she's your sister-in-law and see if you still like her."

"Vivian? Marry Blake?" He sat up abruptly, staggered. "Where did you come by that piece of utter nonsense?"

"It isn't nonsense," she told him, sulking. "She's just his style. Beautiful, sophisticated and blond."

"That's his taste, all right. But do you really think he's got marriage on his mind?" he asked with a wry grin. "That *isn't* his style."

"Maybe she's something special," she grumbled, hating everything about the woman. She glared into space, hurting in ways she never had before. "She told me that Blake wanted her over here to meet us."

"I know. She's the power behind her father. She controls everything he does, or haven't you noticed her ordering him around?"

She shifted on the bench and crossed her legs. "Blake spends all his time with her. Don't tell me it's just for business reasons," she replied, smoothing the close-fitting designer jeans over her thighs. Her eyes dropped to her cream-colored cowboy boots and she grimaced at a scuff on the toe.

"You and I spend a lot of time together, too," he reminded her. "But we're just friends."

She sighed. "That's true."

"And Blake hates it."

Her eyes jerked up. "What?"

He grinned. "He's jealous," he laughed.

She went cherry pink and averted her gaze. "You're nuts!"

"Am I? He's crazily possessive about you. He always has been, but in the past few days I'm almost afraid to sit beside you when he's at home."

She felt her heart racing at the words. She hoped against hope that they were true, even while she knew they weren't. "He's just the domineering type," she corrected nervously.

"Really? Is that why he deliberately picked a fight with your boyfriend to send him packing?" Phillip eyed her narrowly. "When we got home from Charleston, Blake was gone and you were hiding in your room with a headache. What happened between you two while we were gone?"

The blush went all the way to her toes. She couldn't answer him.

"You light up when he walks into a room," he continued, smiling. "And he watches you when he thinks no one's noticing. Like a big, hungry panther with its eyes on a tasty young gazelle."

She hadn't known that, and her heart went wild. "Oh, Phil, does he, really?" she asked involuntarily, and everything she felt was in the starved look in the soft eyes she lifted to his.

He nodded quietly, studying her. "That's just what I thought," he said gently. "Adding your heart to the string he drags behind him, kitten?"

"Is it so obvious?" she sighed miserably. She turned her attention to the passersby.

"To me, because we've always been close," he replied. "I knew why you bought that sexy dress even before you did. You wanted to see what effect it would have on Blake. Dynamite, wasn't it, girl?" he asked knowingly, with a teasing smile.

She flushed wildly. "Do you hide behind the curtains?" she whispered, embarrassed by his perception.

"I'm not in my adolescence, Kate," he reminded her. "You and Blake have always been passionate with each other. You push him hard—it isn't hard to guess at the reaction you get. Blake's not a gentle man."

How little he knew his brother, she thought, her mind going back longingly to that lazy morning in the gazebo...

"Or is he?" he whispered, reading her dreamy expression.

She glared at him. "Don't pry."

"I'm not trying to mind your business," he said gently. "But I don't want to see you end up the loser. Blake's a very experienced man. He may be tempted by a bud about to blossom, but he's shy of nets. Don't try to cut your teeth on him. You might as well try to build a fence around the wind."

"What you really mean is that I can't compete with Her Ladyship," she threw at him.

"That's exactly what I mean," he said with gentle compassion. He patted her hand where it lay on the wood bench. "Kathryn, an experienced woman can attract a man in ways that an inexperienced one wouldn't even think of. I don't want to see you hurt. But you must know you're no competition for Vivian."

"Who said I was trying to be?" she asked. Her face shuttered. "You make Blake sound like a..."

"Blake is my brother," he reminded her. "And I'd do anything for him. But he's just noticed what a delicious little thing you've grown into, and he's lost his bearings. It won't take him long to find them, but that tiny space of time could be enough to destroy you." He squeezed her hand and grimaced. "Love him as a brother. But not as a man. I don't have to tell you how Blake feels about love."

She felt the life draining out of her. Her shoulders slumped, and she nodded weakly. "He doesn't believe in it," she whispered shakily.

"Blake wants one thing from a woman," he said. "And he can't have it from you."

She smiled wistfully. "He wouldn't take it even if I offered," she said quietly, darting a look at him.

"Not deliberately," he agreed. "But you could make him forget every scruple he has, little one. Or didn't you know that men are particularly vulnerable to women they want?"

She sighed softly. "And Blake being Blake, he'd marry me, wouldn't he? Even though he hated the idea of it, and me, he'd do the honorable thing."

"That's exactly what I mean." He held her hand gently. "Nothing would make me happier than to see you happily married to my brother. But I know Blake too well, and so do you. He's too much a cynic to change overnight."

"You don't think he could...care for a woman?" she asked haltingly.

He shrugged. "Blake is a private man. I've lived with him all my life, but there are depths to him that

I've never been allowed to explore. Perhaps he's capable of love. But I think in a way he's afraid of it. He's afraid of being vulnerable." He glanced at her with a dry smile. "He may marry eventually to provide Greyoaks with an heir. He may even fall in love. I don't know."

"You said he was possessive of me," she reminded him.

"Naturally, he's taken care of you half your life," he said. "But what he really feels, no one knows."

She bit her lower lip and nodded, turning away to stare at the pavement. "You're right, of course." She forced a smile to her frozen face. "Let's go get an ice-cream cone."

He caught her arm gently and kept her from getting up. "I'm sorry," he said suddenly. "I didn't mean to hurt you."

"What makes you think you have?" she asked with a smile that was too bright.

"You're in love with him."

She felt her face go white. She was only just beginning to admit that to herself. But, confronted with the accusation, she found she couldn't deny it. Her mouth tried to form words, but her tongue wouldn't cooperate.

He read the confusion in her face and stood up. "Ice cream. Right. What flavor would you like, Kathy...vanilla or strawberry?"

It was only two days until Blake planned to fly them to St. Martin. The pace at the office was hectic. Kathryn took dictation until her fingers felt numb, and Blake's temper, always formidable, seemed to be on a permanent hair trigger.

"You know damned well I don't use my middle initial in a signature," he growled at her, slamming the letters she'd just typed down on his desk violently. "Do them over!"

"If you don't like the way I do things," she complained tightly, "why don't you let Vivian come in and work for you?"

"She'd have been in tears by now," he admitted, with a faintly amused smile.

She straightened in the chair beside his desk, crossing her slender legs impatiently in the gray skirt that matched her silk blouse. "Afraid you might tarnish your shining armor?" she asked.

He studied her through a veil of smoke from his cigarette, his dark eyes thoughtful. "There isn't much danger of that happening with you, is there, Kate?" he asked quietly. "You know just about everything there is to know about me, my faults, my habits."

"Do I really know you at all, Blake?" she wondered absently. "Sometimes you seem very much a stranger."

He lifted his cigarette to his mouth. "Like that day in the gazebo, Kate?" he asked softly, watching the burst of color that shot into her face.

Her eyes darted back to her pad, and her heart ran away. "I don't know what you want from me anymore, Blake."

He got up and moved in front of her, leaning down to catch her chin in his big hand and lift her face up to his piercing gaze. "Maybe that works both ways," he said gruffly. "You're very young, Kathryn Mary."

"Oh, yes, compared to you, I'm a mere child," she returned.

"Little spitting kitten," he chided. Something wild and dangerous smoldered in his eyes. "Would you hiss and claw if I made love to you, Kathryn, or would you purr?"

She caught her breath sharply. "Neither!"

His eyes glittered down at her. "You don't think I could teach you to purr, Kate? Your mouth was wild under mine that day. I can still taste it, even now."

"I . . . didn't know what I was doing," she whispered weakly, embarrassed at the memory of her abandoned response.

"Neither did I, really," he murmured absently, watching her mouth with a disturbingly intense scrutiny. "I touched you and every sane thought went out of my head. All I wanted to do was make love to you until I stopped aching."

She caught her breath, meeting his eyes squarely. It was like the impact of lightning striking. It had been that way for her, too, but all he was admitting to was a purely physical attraction—just as Phillip had warned her. He'd lost his head out of desire, not love.

"Doesn't Vivian make you ache?" she asked in a tight voice, hurting with the certainty that what she felt for him was hopeless.

He searched her eyes quietly. "Not that way."

She dropped her gaze to her lap. "You can always find a woman, Blake," she choked.

He leaned down, placing his hands on either side of her against the chair arms, the curling smoke from his cigarette pungent in her nostrils.

"Not one like you, honey," he growled. "Or are you going to try to convince me that you've ever let another man touch you the way I did?"

She felt the heat creeping up from her throat, and her eyes riveted themselves to his tie, remembering the feel of his hands on her bare back, slightly rough, expertly caressing.

"You were afraid, because it was the first time. But if I'd insisted on making love to you, you wouldn't have stopped me. We both know that."

She felt the embarrassment, like a living thing, and she hated him for what he could do to her with words. He made her vulnerable. She'd never been vulnerable to any man before, it was new and disconcerting, and to cover her fear she sought refuge in temper.

"You flatter yourself, don't you?" she asked crisply, raising her sparkling eyes to his. "Maybe I was experimenting, Blake, did you think about that?" She watched the darkness grow in his eyes. "What makes you think I don't feel exactly that way with other men?"

"What other men?" he shot at her. "Phillip?"

She tore her eyes away and stared down at her pad blankly. There was suppressed fury in his voice, and she knew better than to deliberately goad him. If he touched her, she'd go crazy. It was her basic reaction to that vibrant masculinity that rippled in every hard muscle of his body. She was too vulnerable now, and the only way to keep him from seeing it was to make sure she kept him at arm's length.

"We'd better get this work out of the way," he said coolly, and sat down behind his desk again, idly crushing out his cigarette. "How about that shipment of poly-cotton we never received from our Georgia mill?" he asked quietly. "Check with the office there and find out if it was shipped. The spreaders will need it for the next cut."

"Yes, sir," she replied in her best businesslike tone. "Anything else?"

"Yes," he said gruffly, watching her. "Send a dozen red roses to Vivian at the house."

That hit her like a ton of bricks, but she didn't even flinch. Methodically, she made a note on her pad and nodded. "One dozen. I'll call the florist right away. How would you like the card to read?"

He was still eyeing her. "Have them put, 'Thanks for last night' and sign it 'Blake.' Got that?"

"Got it," she replied. Her voice sounded vaguely strangled, but she kept the expression out of her face. "Anything else?"

He swiveled his chair around to stare out the window. "No."

She went out and closed the door quietly behind her. Tears were welling in her eyes by the time she got back to her own desk.

Eight

"Just imagine, a week in St. Martin," Maude sighed, studying the list of chores she'd outlined for Mrs. Johnson and the daily maids while the family was away. "How sweet of Blake to take us all with him, especially when he's getting along so well with Vivian!"

"Oh, it's delightful," Kathryn agreed dully.

"They've hardly been apart at all," she sighed. "And they do make such a striking pair, Blake so dark and Vivian so fair.... I think he's really serious this time." She clasped her slender hands together and beamed. "I'd love to plan a spring wedding. We could decorate the house with orchids..."

"Excuse me, Maude, but I really have to start getting my things together," Kathryn said brightly, rising from the sofa. "You don't mind?"

Maude was deep in her plans. "No, dear, go right ahead," she mumbled absently.

Kathryn went up the winding staircase, feeling dead inside. As she passed by Vivian's room, her eye was caught by the vase full of red roses sitting on the dresser in full view of the open door. Vivian had done that deliberately, no doubt, and Kathryn felt as if she'd been shot. At least Blake hadn't suspected how she felt about him. That would have been unbearable, especially since he was taking such a sudden and intense interest in the seductive blonde. They were going nightclubbing together, later that evening, and they'd been locked up in Blake's study ever since dinner. As had happened so many times since her return to Greyoaks, Kathryn sought out Phillip for companionship. And that seemed to catch Blake's attention in the most violent way.

The following morning he found Phillip sitting on her desk and he seemed to erupt.

"Don't you have anything to do, Phillip?" he growled at his younger brother.

"Why, yes, I do," Phillip replied.

"Then why the hell don't you go and do it?" came the terse, irritable question.

Phillip stood erect, his hands in his pockets, and studied the bigger, older man quietly, frowning. "I was asking Kate to take in a movie with me tonight," he said. "Any objections?"

Blake's jaw tautened. "Make your dates at home. Not on my time."

"I do have an interest in the corporation," Phillip reminded him. "Just like all the other stockholders."

"Try acting like it," Blake said coldly. His eyes darted to Kathryn. "Bring your pad. I've got some letters to dictate." He went back into his office and roughly closed the door.

Phillip stared after him, not taking offense at all. He knew Blake too well. A slow smile flared on his lips. "Now, in a lesser man, I'd swear that was jealousy," he teased, eyeing Kathryn.

She stood up with a sigh, clutching her steno pad to her chest. "But not in a man with someone like Vivian practically engaged to him," she reminded him. "We'd better get to work before he gives us a pink slip."

He shrugged. "With the temper he's been in lately, I'm not sure it wouldn't be a relief."

"Speaking of relief," she said, lowering her voice, "you promised to help me look for an apartment."

"Not until we get back from St. Martin," he said stubbornly. "And only then if Blake's temper improves. I don't have a suicidal bone in my body, Kate, and I'm not taking on Blake for you."

She sighed. "You won't have to," she said bitterly. "He'll be glad to see me go now, and you know it."

He studied her. "Will he, really?" he murmured.

"Kathryn!" Blake thundered over the intercom.

She flinched and hurried into his office.

He was sitting behind his desk, leaning back in his chair, and he glared at her when she walked in.

"From now on, don't encourage Phillip to waste time talking to you during working hours," he said without preamble, his eyes blazing. "I don't pay either of you to socialize."

She stared at him belligerently. "Do I have to have your permission to say good morning to him now?" she wanted to know.

"In this building, yes," he replied curtly. His dark eyes held hers fiercely. "You practically live in each other's pockets already. I shouldn't think it would work a hardship for you to spend just eight hours away from him!"

He whipped his chair forward and grabbed up a letter, his leonine face as hard as the oak desk under his powerful hands. She remembered without wanting to the warmth and tenderness of those hard fingers on her bare skin . . .

"Are you ready?" he asked curtly.

She sat down quickly, positioning her pad on her lap. "Any time you are," she said in her most professional tone.

For the rest of the day, Kathryn and Blake maintained a cool politeness between them that raised eyebrows among the staff. There had been numerous arguments, ever since Kathryn's appointment as his secretary, but this was different. Now they were avoiding each other completely. They didn't argue, because there was no contact between them.

"I say, have you and Blake had a falling out?" Vivian asked Kathryn that evening as she waited for Blake to change for their dinner date. "You've hardly spoken to each other for the past couple of days."

Kathryn, curled up on the sofa in her ivory-colored jumpsuit with a book, glanced at the older woman coolly. The blue Qiana dress the actress was wearing left nothing to the imagination, and even Kathryn had to admit it flattered her figure, her lovely face, and her elegantly coiffured blond hair. Just Blake's style, she thought bitterly.

"Not at all," Kathryn replied finally. "Blake and I were never close," she lied, remembering happier times when there was never a cross word between them, and Blake's eyes were tender.

"Oh, really?" Vivian probed. She smiled a little haughtily, primping at a mirror on the wall between two elegant bronze sconces. "I do hope you and I will get on together. Living in the same house, you know..." She let her voice trail away insinuatingly.

"Have you set a date?" Kathryn asked with careful unconcern.

"Not quite," the blonde replied. "But it won't be long."

"I'm delighted for both of you," she murmured as she stared blankly at her book.

"Are you ready, darling?" Vivian gushed as Blake came into the room. "I'm simply famished!"

"Let's go, then," he replied with a sensuous note in his voice that Kathryn didn't miss. But she didn't raise her eyes from the book, didn't look at him or speak to him. She felt dead, frozen. It wasn't until the door slammed behind them that she was able to relax. How fortunate, she thought, that Dick Leeds and Maude had also gone out for the night, and that she'd convinced Phillip to go to the movies alone.

There was no one to watch her cry. Now, for certain, she'd have to leave Greyoaks. There was no way she could live in it with Vivian.

The following day dawned bright and sunny, perfect for their flight to St. Martin. Kathryn and Phillip were bringing up the rear. Vivian, in a stunning white lace pantsuit, was clinging to Blake's arm like ivy while Dick Leeds and Maude followed along deep in conversation. Kathryn was wearing a simple peasant dress in green and brown patterns that brought out the deep green of her eyes and set off her long, waving dark hair. She was dressed for comfort, not for style, and she knew she was no competition for the blonde. She wasn't trying to be. She'd lost Blake, even though she'd never really had a chance to win him. There were too many years between them.

"You're tearing at my heart," Phillip said quietly, watching her as she watched Blake and Vivian.

She lifted her sad eyes to his. "Why?"

"I've never seen a woman love a man the way you love Blake," he replied quietly, with none of his usual gaiety.

She lifted her shoulders in a careless gesture. "I'll get over it," she murmured. "It...it's just going to take a little time, that's all. I'll land on my feet, Phil."

He caught her hand and held it gently as they walked toward the small jet owned by the corporation. "I honestly thought it was infatuation, at first," he admitted gently. "But I'm beginning to realize just how wrong I was. You'd do anything for him, wouldn't you? Even stand aside and watch him marry another woman, as long as he was happy."

Her long eyelashes curled down onto her cheeks. "Isn't that what love is all about?" she asked in a soft whisper. "I want him to be happy." Her eyes closed briefly. "I want everything for him."

He squeezed her hand. "Stiff upper lip, darling," he said under his breath. "Don't let him see you suffer."

She forced a laugh through her tight throat. "Oh, of course not," she said brightly. "We revolutionaries are very tough, you know."

"That's my girl. But why are you giving up the battle so soon?"

"Who said I was giving up?" she asked, glancing at him. "I've got the job I wanted, but not the apartment. Just wait until we come back!"

He chuckled. "That's my girl. I knew you could work it out."

"Of course we can," she said with a gleeful smile.

"We?" he asked, apprehensive.

"You know lots of people in real estate," she reminded him. "I'm sure you can find me something I can afford. In a good neighborhood."

"Now, just a minute, Kathy..."

But she was already boarding the plane.

The executive jet was roomy and comfortable, and as long as Kathryn didn't look out the window of the pressurized cabin, she was fine. She'd never gotten over the bouts with airsickness that were a carryover from her childhood, despite Blake's expert handling of the airplane.

Vivian was sitting in the co-pilot's seat, for which Kathryn was eternally grateful. She couldn't have borne her haughty company, her gloating smile.

"You look very pale, dear," Maude said sympathetically, reaching out to pat Kathryn's cold hand. "How about an airsick pill?"

"I've already had two," came the subdued reply. "All they do is make me dizzy."

"A spot of brandy might help," Dick Leeds suggested gently, as he appeared briefly beside her.

She shook her head, feeling even more nauseated. "I'll be all right," she assured them.

"Lie down for a while," Phillip said as the older passengers moved away. "Take off your shoes and just sleep," he coaxed, helping her stretch out in one of the plush, comfortable seats. "We'll be there before you know it."

They landed at Queen Juliana airport on Sint Maarten—the Dutch side of the divided island. As they stepped out onto the ground, the first thing Kathryn noticed was the hot, moist air that enveloped her. She stared at the blue skies and palm trees and the flags flying proudly at the terminal. She remembered the island with pleasure, as she had stayed many times at the family's villa.

A customs official took their immigration cards, and their passports, with a minimum of fuss. Blake obtained a rental car, and they were on their way.

"Where is your house?" Vivian asked, staring out at the red-roofed homes they passed as they drove along the paved road.

"On St. Martin," Blake replied as he drove. "The French side of the island, which is, by the way, very French. The Dutch side, which we're in now, tends to be more Americanized."

"It's confusing," Vivian laughed.

"Not really," Maude told her. "One gets used to it. The division is political as well as lingual, but the people are delightful on both sides of the island. And you'll love the shops in Marigot—that's very near our villa."

"And the restaurants," Phillip grinned. "You've never had better seafood."

"What do you like about it, darling?" Vivian asked Blake.

"The peace and quiet," he replied.

"Which you don't find much of during peak tourist season," Phillip laughed.

"Well, this is hurricane season, not tourist season," Maude said, shivering at the thought. "I do hope we don't run into any rough weather."

"Amen," Blake said with a faint smile. "I've got to fly over to Haiti on business while we're here."

"What for?" Vivian asked with blunt curiosity.

Blake gave her a lazy sidelong look. "I might have a woman stashed away there," he said.

It was the first time Kathryn had ever seen Vivian blush, and she made a good job of it. Her pale face turned a bright pink. "Oh, look, cattle!" she said quickly, gazing out the window toward a green meadow nestled between mountains.

Blake only chuckled, concentrating on the road as they passed from the Dutch side of the island to the French.

Maude jumped as they hit a pothole. "Oh, you can always tell when we pass into St. Martin," she moaned. "The roads over here are just terrible!"

"Just like home, isn't it?" Phillip asked, winking at Kathryn.

"I think we have very good roads at home, Phillip," Maude said, "an excellent county commission and a superb road department. Remember, darling, I helped Jeff Brown get appointed to the state highway board, and I think he's done a fine job."

"Forgive me for that unthinking comment," Phillip pleaded. "Heaven forbid that I should sully the name..."

"Oh, do be quiet," Maude moaned. "Vivian, here's Marigot," she said, pointing out the window toward the bay where fishing boats dotted the Baie de Marigot past the powdery beach. There were red-roofed houses stretching all the way down the beach, thick in places, mingling with hotels. Kathryn felt a shiver of girlish excitement as they stopped at one of them minutes later. It was Maison Baie—roughly, Bay House—and her eyes lovingly traced the white stone building with its graceful wrought-iron balconies and breezeways and long windows. It, too, had the classic red roof, and carved wood doors.

"Is this yours?" Vivian asked, her eyes also taking in the graceful lines of the house and its colorful setting with palm trees, bougainvillea, and sea-grape trees farther out on the powder-fine sand.

"Yes," Blake replied, cutting the engine. "Maison Baie. It's been in the family since my father was a boy, and the second generation of caretakers—a retired sea captain named Rouget and his wife—live here year round, looking after it."

"It's very pretty," Vivian said enthusiastically.

Kathryn stayed beside Phillip, feeling the coolness of the house wash over her as they walked inside. Rouget, a tall, thin man with white hair, came to meet them, welcoming them in his native French. Blake replied, his accent faultless, and Kathryn had to work to keep up with the translation. She'd forgotten just how French this side of the island really was. Her rusty attempts to speak the language had always amused Blake. Glancing at him, she wondered if anything she did would ever amuse him again.

The look on her young face was revealing, and Phillip drew her away before Blake could see it. She smiled at him gratefully as they left the spacious living room to settle into their respective rooms. Already she was hoping the visit would be a brief one.

That afternoon Vivian persuaded Blake to take her back to Marigot to look in the shops. Maude and Dick Leeds, deciding that the sun was a bit much, lounged on the balcony with chilled burgundy provided by Rouget. Kathryn spent the rest of the day lying quietly in bed, feeling out of sorts. The combination of the flight and the sultry, tropical climate had put her flat on her back. When night came, she was barely aware of Maude's fingers gently shaking her.

"Darling, we're going into Marigot to have seafood. Do you feel like coming with us?" she asked.

Kathryn sat up, surprised to find that the nausea and weariness were completely gone. "Of course," she said, smiling. "Just give me a minute to change..."

"What's wrong with what you have on?" Blake asked from the doorway, and she felt his dark eyes sliding up and down her slender body in the peasant dress that had ridden up above her knees while she rested. She pulled it down quickly and, smoothing it nervously, got to her feet.

"I...I suppose it would do, if we're not going anywhere fancy."

"The restaurant isn't formal, Kathryn," he said, moving inside the room. "Still queasy?" he added gently.

That soft note in his voice almost brought tears to her eyes. She turned away to pick up her brush. "No," she replied. "I'm all right. Just let me run a brush through my hair."

"Don't be long," Maude teased. "I feel as if I haven't eaten for days."

Kathryn nodded, expecting Blake to go, too. But he didn't. He closed the door quietly, an action that made Kathryn's heart go wild. She watched him in the mirror.

He moved up behind her, his dark eyes holding hers in the glass, so close that she could feel the blazing warmth of his big body. He was dressed in a red and white patterned tropical shirt, open at the throat, revealing a sensuous glimpse of curling dark hair and bronzed flesh. His slacks were white, hugging the powerful lines of his thighs. She could hardly drag her eyes away from him.

"Do you really feel up to this?" he asked quietly. "If you don't, I'll stay home with you."

The concern in his deep voice would have been heaven, if it had been meant differently. But it was the compassion of a man for a child, not of a man for his woman.

"I always get airsick," she reminded him dully. "I'm all right, Blake."

"Are you?" he asked tightly. "The light's gone out of you."

"It's been . . . a long week," she whispered unsteadily.

He nodded, dropping his narrow gaze to her long hair, her shoulders. His big hands went to her waist, testing the softness of her flesh through the thin dress, rough and vaguely caressing.

"I...I think we all needed a vacation," she laughed nervously. The feel of his hands made her heart turn over in her chest.

"Yes." He drew her slowly back against his big, hard-muscled body, so that she could feel his breath against her hair. "You're trembling," he said in a deep, lazy tone.

Her eyes closed. Her hands went involuntarily to rest on top of his as he slid them closer around her waist. "I know," she managed weakly.

His fingers contracted painfully. "Kate..."

She couldn't help herself. Her head dropped back against his broad chest and her body openly yielded to him. In the mirror, she watched his dark, broad hands move slowly, seductively up her waist until they cupped her high breasts over the green and brown pattern of the low-cut peasant dress. She let him touch her, helpless in his embrace, the hardness of his thighs pressing into the back of her legs as he moved even closer.

His dark eyes held hers in the mirror, watching her reaction. His cheek brushed against the top of her head, ruffling the soft dark hair while his fingers brushed and stroked, the action even more erotic because she could watch it happening.

Her fingers came up to rest on top of his, pressing them closer to the soft curves, while her heart threatened to choke her with its furious thudding.

His face moved down and she felt the heat of his lips at the side of her neck brushing, teasing, his tongue lightly tracing the line of it down to her shoulder.

"You smell of flowers," he whispered. His hands moved up and under the low neckline to surge down and capture her taut, bare breasts.

She moaned helplessly and bit her lip to stifle the sound that must surely have passed even through the thick stone walls of the house.

"I wish to God we were alone, Kate," he whispered huskily. "I'd lie down with you on that bed over there and before I was through, you'd be biting back more than one sweet moan. You'd be biting me," he whispered seductively, while his hands made magic on her arching body. "Clawing me, begging me to do more than touch your breasts."

"Blake . . ." she moaned, with a throb in her voice that broke the sound in the middle of his name.

She whirled in his arms, rising against his big body, her arms going around his neck, her lips parted and pleading.

"Kiss me," she whispered, trembling. "Blake, Blake, kiss me hard...!"

"How hard?" he whispered huskily as he bent. His mouth bit at hers sensuously, lightly bruising, open, taunting. "Like that?"

"No," she whispered. She went on tiptoe, her green eyes misty with mindless hunger, her lips parted as she caught his head and brought his open mouth down on hers. Her tongue darted into his mouth and she withdrew tauntingly just a half-breath away. "Like that..."

His mouth crushed hers, his tongue exploring the line of her lips, thrusting past them in to the warm darkness of her mouth, his arms contracting so strongly that they brought the length of her body close enough to feel every hardening line of his.

"Do you...want me?" she whispered achingly.

"God in heaven, can't you feel it?" he ground out. "Stop asking silly questions...closer, Kate," he whispered. "Move your body against mine. Stroke it against me..."

She eased up on tiptoe. "Like this, Blake?" she whispered shakily.

His mouth bit at hers. "Harder than that," he murmured. "I can't feel you."

Trembling, she repeated the arousing action and felt a small shudder go through his powerful body.

"Do you like this?" she managed in a stranger's seductive voice.

"Let me show you how much I like it," he whispered. He bent and lifted her off the floor, looking down into her green eyes as he started toward the huge mahogany posted bed against the wall.

Her arms clung to him, her lips answering the suddenly tender kisses he was brushing against her lips, her eyelids, her eyebrows, her cheeks. The chaste touch of his mouth was at odds with the heavy, hard shudder of his heartbeat against her body, the harsh sigh of his breath that betrayed the emotions he was experiencing.

"Are you going to make love to me?" she whispered against his lips, knowing in her heart even as she asked the question that she was going to give him everything he wanted.

"Do you want me to, Kate?" he whispered back. "Are you afraid?"

"How could I be afraid of you?" she managed in a tight voice. "When I . . ." Before she could get the confession out, before she could tell him how desperately she loved him, there was a sharp, harsh knock on the door, and he jerked involuntarily.

Vivian's abrasive voice called, "Blake, are you there? We're starving!"

"My God, so am I," he whispered, and the eyes that met Kathryn's as he set her back on her feet were blazing with unsatisfied desire.

She moved unsteadily away from him, her heart jerking wildly, her breath coming in uneven little gasps. She went back to the mirror and picked up a lipstick, applying it to her swollen mouth while Blake took a steadying breath and went to answer the door.

"I'm so hungry, darling," Vivian murmured with a smile, her hawklike eyes catching the slight swell of his lower lip, the unruly hair that Kathryn's fingers had tangled lightly. "Can't we go to dinner now that you're through talking to sweet little Kate?"

"I'm hungry myself," Kathryn said, avoiding Blake's eyes as she edged out the door past him, managed a tight smile in Vivian's direction, and almost ran from the room. What in heaven's name had possessed her to allow Blake such liberties? Now the fat was really going to be in the fire. She had let him know how desperately she wanted him, and she was afraid that he'd take advantage of it. What Phillip had said was true—Blake could lose his head. If he did, he'd be gentleman enough to marry her. But she didn't want Blake on those terms. She only wanted his love, not a forced marriage. What was she going to do?

* * *

The little French restaurant was as familiar to
Kathryn as Maison Baie, and she remembered the
owners well—a French couple from Martinique who
served the most delicious lobster soufflé and crêpes
flambées Kathryn had ever tasted. Her appetite came
back the instant she saw the food, and Phillip's
pleasant company at her elbow made it even more
palatable.

She avoided Blake's piercing gaze all through the
meal and when they got back to the house, she
quickly excused herself and went to bed.

That night set the pattern for the next two days.
Blake wore a perpetual scowl at Kathryn's nervous
avoidance of him, and Phillip's efforts to play
peacemaker met with violence on Blake's part. He
stayed away during the day with Vivian, taking her
on tours of nearby Saba and St. Eustatius—known
to the locals as "Statia." But in the evenings he and
the slinky blonde stayed close to home while he dis-
cussed the mill problem with Dick Leeds. It was at
the end of one of these endless discussions that
Kathryn accidentally came across him in the deserted hall upstairs.

His dark eyes narrowed angrily as she froze in
front of him, on her way to change for supper in
Marigot.

"Still running away from me?" he asked scathingly.

"I'm not running," she replied unsteadily.

"Like hell you're not," he returned gruffly. "You practically dive under things to keep out of my way lately. What's wrong, Kathryn, do you think you're so damned irresistible that I can't keep my hands off you?"

"Of course not!" she gasped.

"Then why go to so much trouble to avoid me?" he persisted.

She drew a slow, steady breath. "Phillip and I have been busy, that's all," she managed.

His face tightened. A cold, cruel smile touched his hard mouth. "Busy? So you finally decided to taste the wine, did you, honey?" His voice drew blood. "It's just as well. You're too much of a baby for me, Kathryn. I hate like hell to rob cradles!"

He turned on his heel and left her standing there.

She couldn't bear for Blake to think that about her, to look at her with eyes so full of contempt they made her shiver. But what could she do? The impact of his anger made her reckless and when the delicious white wine was passed around at the restaurant that night, she had more than her share of refills. Throwing caution to the wind, she sipped and swallowed until all her heartaches seemed to vanish.

When Blake announced that he was flying to Haiti the next morning, she barely heard him. Her mind was far away, on pleasant thoughts.

"Honey, you're drunk," Phillip said with some concern when they got back to the villa. "Go to bed and sleep it off, huh?"

She smiled at him lazily. "I'm not sleepy."

"Pretend, before you give Vivian something else to laugh about," he asked softly. "And don't push Blake's temper any further tonight. I'm surprised he hasn't lectured you about the amount of wine you drank. He didn't like it, that's for sure."

"Be a pet and stop preaching," she murmured, fanning herself with one hand. "It's so hot!"

"Feels like storm weather," he agreed. "Go to bed. You'll cool off."

She shrugged and, to Phillip's quiet relief, went up to her room before the others came inside the house.

Nine

———

But once she got into bed, she was only hotter. It was too sultry, too quiet, and her thoughts began to haunt her. Blake's harsh words came back like a persistent mosquito—too much of a baby, he said. *Too much of a baby.*

She tossed and turned until it became unbearable. Finally she got up, put on her brief white bikini and grabbed up a beach towel. If she couldn't sleep, she might as well cool off in the bay. Just the thought of the cold water made her feel better.

She made her way downstairs in the dark house with the ease of long practice, and walked a little unsteadily out onto the beach. Her bare feet smarted on the grainy pebbles until she reached the softer sand where the foaming surf curled lazily. The air was static, the beach completely deserted. She stood and breathed in the delicious scent of blooming flowers that merged with the tangy sea smell.

"What are you doing out here?" came a harsh, deep voice from the shelter of a nearby palm.

She watched Blake move into view in the moonlight, wearing a pair of white shorts and the same red and white patterned silk shirt he'd been wearing the other night. Only tonight it was unbuttoned all the way down his massive chest.

"I asked you a question," he said, and even in the moonlight she could see the boldness in his dark eyes as they sketched her slender body in its brief white covering. The way he was looking at her made her pulses pound.

"I came out for a swim," she said, very carefully enunciating each word. "I'm hot."

"Are you?"

Her eyes traced the hard lines of his body, lingering on his massive chest with its wedge of dark, curling hair that disappeared below his waistline. Her lips parted as she felt a surge of longing so great, it moved her toward him without her even being aware of it until she was close enough to touch him.

"Don't be angry with me," she pleaded in a husky voice. Her fingers went to his broad chest, touching the bronzed skin nervously, feeling the sensuous masculinity in those muscles that clenched under her soft touch.

"Don't," he said harshly, catching her hands roughly.

"Why not, Blake?" she asked recklessly. "Don't you like for me to touch you? I'm just a baby, remember," she taunted, moving her fingers under his deliberately. She could feel his heartbeat quicken until it was heavy and hard, hear the rough intake of his breath as she moved closer and let her body rest against him. The naked brush of her thighs against the hair-roughened muscles of his was intoxicating, and the feel of his hard chest against the softness of her body caused her to sigh.

"Blake," she whispered achingly. The alcohol she'd consumed made her uninhibited; she'd never been so dangerously relaxed with him before. But now she touched his shoulders and the muscles of his big arms in a desperate surge of longing, drowning in the nearness of him, the feel of his big, warm body under her exploring hands.

Her head moved forward, and she pressed her mouth against his chest, drinking in the tang of his cologne and the smell of some spicy soap on his bare skin.

He caught his breath sharply, and his hands suddenly gripped her bare waist. "Don't, Kate," he whispered roughly. "You'll make me do something we'll both regret. You don't know what you're doing to me!"

Her body moved sensuously against his, and she heard the hard groan that broke from his throat. "I know," she moaned, lifting her face to meet his blazing eyes. "Oh, Blake, love me!"

"On a public beach?" he growled huskily, before bending his head to take her mouth.

Her arms lifted around his neck, and his hands dropped to her thighs, lifting her body abruptly against his so that it was molded to every masculine line of him in a joining that tore a moan from her lips. His fingers contracted, and she felt the shudder rip through his body with the force of a blow, felt the arms holding her begin to tremble as his mouth invaded hers, devouring it in the silence of the night.

They swayed together like palm trees in a hurricane, tasting, touching, burning with a hunger that seemed incapable of satisfaction. Her fingers buried themselves in his thick, dark hair, ruffling it as she yielded to the violent passion she'd aroused.

She felt his fingers at the strings that held her bikini top in place, and she was too lost in him to notice what was happening until she felt with a sense of wonder the curling hair of his chest against the bare softness of her own, and she cried out with pleasure.

"This is how it felt that day in the gazebo, isn't it, Kate?" he breathed roughly at her ear as he pressed her breasts against the thickness of the dark hair that matted his muscular chest. "I want all of you against me like this, I want to lie down on the beach with you and let you feel every delicious difference between your body and mine."

Her thighs trembled where his broad fingers caressed them, drawing her hips to his. Her nails bit deeply into his hard back and she sobbed at the wave of emotion that trembled over her weak body.

"Kate, Kathy, sweet, sweet love," he whispered as his mouth touched her lips again and again, brief, hard kisses that aroused her almost beyond bearing so that she pressed even closer against his big, warm body and felt the shudder that went through it.

His mouth moved down her throat and her body arched as he found the thrust of her breasts and let his lips brush warmly, moistly, against flesh that had known no man's touch except his.

"Blake," she whispered achingly. I love you, she thought, I love you more than my own life, and if I have nothing else, I'll have this to remember when I'm old, and you and Vivian have children and I'm alone with my memories... Her fingers tangled in his hair and pressed his exploring mouth closer.

"God, you're soft," he breathed, lifting his head at last to move his mouth sensuously over hers. "Soft, like silk, like velvet against my body...Kathy, I want you. I want you like I want air to breathe, I want to make love to you..." His mouth took hers again, deeply possessive, his arms swallowing her, rocking her while the waves pounded rhythmically against the white sand, the sound just penetrating her mind while she got drunker on pleasure than she ever had on wine.

"We've got to stop this," he groaned, dragging his mouth away to look down at her in the darkness that wasn't darkness at all, his eyes black and tortured as they met hers. "I can't take you here!"

Her hands ran lovingly over his hair-matted chest, feeling the roughness of it, the strength of those well-developed muscles. She wanted to touch all of him, every sensuous inch of him.

"We could go inside," she suggested in a husky whisper.

"Yes, we could," he said roughly. "And you'd wake in my arms hating me. Not like this, Kate. Damn it, not like this!"

He pushed her away, and for just an instant, his eyes possessed the small high curve of her breasts like a thirsty man gulping water. Then he swooped and retrieved the bikini top. He dropped it into her shaking hands and turned his back.

"Put it on," he said harshly. His fingers dug into his shirt pocket for his crushed cigarette package and matches. "Let me cool off for a minute. My God, Kate, do you see what you do to me?" he growled, half-laughing as his fingers fumbled with the cigarette.

She tied the top back in place with trembling fingers, avoiding his direct gaze. Out of the corner of her eye, she saw the orange tip of his cigarette glow suddenly as he took a draw from it.

"I'm sorry, Blake," she said miserably. "I...I didn't mean to...to..."

"It's all right, Kate," he said gently. "You had too much to drink, that's all."

Her eyes closed and she folded her arms around her trembling body. "I'm so ashamed," she ground out.

He stiffened. "Ashamed?"

She turned away. "I can't think what got into me," she laughed harshly. "Maybe it's my age, maybe I'm going through my second childhood."

"Or maybe you're just plain damned frustrated," he said, a whip in his deep voice. "Is that it, Kate? Can't Phillip give you what you need?"

Shocked, she turned, lifting her puzzled eyes to his across the distance. She'd never seen his face so hard. "What?"

He laughed shortly. "You make no secret of your preference for his company, honey," he reminded her. "But he isn't passionate. You're just finding that out, aren't you? Can't he satisfy those wild hungers in you, Kate? Can't he give you what I can?"

"I don't... I don't feel that way about Phil," she stammered.

"Don't expect me to stand in for him again," he shot back. "I draw the line at being used for a damned substitute."

"But I wasn't...!"

He turned away. "Go back inside and sober up," he said, stripping off his shirt.

She stared after him, watching as he walked forward, flicking the cigarette away, and abruptly dived into the moonlit water.

Kathryn wanted desperately to follow him, to make him understand how she felt. To tell him that

she loved him, not Phillip, that she'd give anything
to be to him what Vivian was. But she knew he'd
never listen to her in his present mood. He might
never listen to her again, regardless of his mood. She
wanted to hit herself for putting away all that wine.
She'd killed Blake's respect for her, and along with
it, every chance she'd ever had of making him love
her. With a sigh, she turned away and picked up her
beach towel. She trailed it aimlessly behind her as she
walked past the gnarled sea-grape trees back to the
house, the flower-scented breeze making sultry
whispers at her ear.

She overslept the next morning, and when she
awoke it was with a bursting headache. She got to her
feet to get an aspirin, glancing toward the rain-
blasted window and the darkness of the clouds.

Phillip was the only one in the living room when
she went downstairs.

"Where is everybody?" she asked, lifting a hand
to her throbbing head as she sat down with the coffee she'd poured herself from the tray in front of the
sofa.

"They drove Blake to the airport," he replied,
watching her closely. "He was bent on flying to Haiti
today, despite the storm warnings. He left before this
started; I guess they stopped to do some shopping on
the way back."

Her eyes stared blankly out the window at the pouring rain, whipped by the wind. "It looks bad out there," she remarked, her heart aching when she remembered what had happened last night and why Blake might have decided to take a risk like this. Had she made him reckless? Had her stupidity caused him to lose his temper so badly that he had to get away from the island, from her, at any cost?

"Yes, it does," he said. He raised his cup of coffee to his lips, watching her over the rim of it. He sipped some of the hot liquid and then abruptly put the cup down with a clatter. "What happened?"

The question was so unexpected that she stared at him for several seconds before she spoke. "What?"

"What happened last night?" he asked again. "Blake looked like a thunderhead when he came downstairs this morning, and he didn't say a word all through breakfast. He didn't ask where you were, but he kept watching the stairs, as if he expected you to come down them any second. He looked like a starving man with his eye on a five-course meal."

Tears formed in her own eyes, ran down her cheeks. She put her cup down and buried her face in her hands, crying brokenly.

He sat down beside her and patted her awkwardly on the shoulder. "What did you do to him, Kathy?"

"I'd had too much to drink," she whispered through her fingers, "and he'd said I was a child—"

"So you went out and proved to him that you weren't," he said softly, smiling at her.

A nagging suspicion formed in the back of her mind and she raised her tear-wet eyes to his with the question in them.

"It's a very public beach, Kathryn Mary," he said with a mischievous grin. "And the moon was out."

"Oh, no," she whispered, going red. She buried her face in her hands a second time. "You saw us."

"Not only me," he replied drily. "Vivian. Watch yourself, little one, I got a look at her face before she stormed off upstairs."

She swallowed. "Did anyone else . . . ?"

He shook his head. "No. Mom and Dick were arguing politics. I'd taken Vivian for a stroll along the porch to see the view . . . and what a view we saw. Whew!"

The blush got hotter. "I could die," she moaned. "I could just die!"

"It's nothing to be embarrassed about," he said gently. "I'd give anything to have a woman care that much about me. And if you wondered how Blake really felt, I imagine you found out."

"I found out that he wants me," she replied miserably. "I knew that before. It's not enough, Phillip."

"How do you know that's all he feels?" he asked quietly. He leaned forward, studying the coffee table. "Blake's deep, Kathryn. He keeps everything to himself."

"I couldn't have faced him this morning," she said bitterly. "Not after what I did. Oh, Phillip, I'll never have another glass of wine as long as I live, I'll never touch another drop."

"Don't give up, girl," he said.

"Phillip, I don't have anything to give up," she reminded him.

"Don't you?" he asked, frowning. "I'm not so sure about that."

Vivian and Kathryn were left alone briefly while Maude supervised the evening meal and Dick and Phillip talked shop on the long porch. The rain had finally vanished, but the wind had only let up a little, and Kathryn couldn't help wondering if Blake was all right. He wasn't due back until the next morning, but that didn't stop her from worrying.

"You really did get smashed last night, didn't you?" Vivian asked, shooting a quick glance at Kathryn's subdued expression as she poured herself a small sherry at the bar.

Kathryn stiffened. "I'm not used to alcohol," she said defensively, eyeing the coffee cup she was holding.

"What a pity you had to overdo it," the blonde said with a pitying glance. "Blake was utterly disgusted."

Her face flamed. "Was he?" she choked.

"I saw you, of course," she sighed. "Poor man, he didn't stand a chance when you absolutely threw yourself at him like that. Any man would be...stirred," she added. Her eyes sharpened. "For my part, I'm furious with you. Blake and I...well, I've told you how things are. And I should think you'd have enough pride not to offer yourself to an engaged man."

The coffee cup crashed to the floor. Kathryn got up and ran for the stairs. She couldn't bear to hear any more.

Blake was due by mid-morning, but when Phillip came back from the airport his face was grim.

"What's wrong? What happened?" Kathryn asked frantically.

"He left Haiti at daylight," Phillip said through tight lips. "And filed a flight plan. But he hasn't been heard from since takeoff." He caught her hand and squeezed it warmly. "They think he's gone down in some rough winds off the coast of Puerto Rico."

Ten

She couldn't remember a time in her life when she'd been so afraid. She paced. She worried. She cried. When Phillip finally took pity on all of them and agreed to let them wait it out at the airport, she hugged him out of sheer relief. At least they'd be a little closer to the communications network.

The airport wasn't crowded, but it wasn't as comfortable as the restaurant in the adjoining motel, so the five of them waited there. Vivian was worried, but it didn't deter her from flirting with Phillip or casting a wandering eye around the restaurant for interested looks. There were several Europeans staying in the motel, and a good many of the customers were men.

Kathryn had eyes for no one. Her worried gaze was fixed on her lap while she tried not to wonder how she could go through life without Blake. She'd never thought about that before. Blake had always seemed invincible, immortal. He was so strong and commanding, it didn't occur to her that he was as vulnerable as any other man. Now, she had to consider that possibility and it froze her very blood.

"I can't stand it," she whispered to Phillip, rising. "I'm going out to the airfield."

"Kathryn, it may be hours," he protested, walking with her as far as the door, only to cast a concerned look back at Maude, who was deep in conversation with Dick Leeds, her thin face drawn and taut with fear.

"I know," she said. She managed a wan little smile. "But if he . . . *when* he comes back," she corrected quickly, "I think one of us should be there."

He clenched her shoulders hard. His face was older, harder. "Kate, it's not definite that he's coming back. You're got to face that. His plane went down, that's absolutely all I know. The rescue crews are searching, but heaven only knows what they'll find!"

She bit her lower lip, hard, and her eyes were misty when she raised them, but her jaw was set stubbornly. "He's alive," she said. "I know he's alive, Phillip."

"Honey..." he began piteously.

"Do you think I'd still be breathing if Blake were dead?" she asked in a wild, choked whisper. "Do you think my heart would be beating?"

He closed his eyes momentarily, as if searching for words.

"I'm going outside," she said gently. She turned and left him there.

The skies were still gray, and the sun hadn't come out. She paced the apron with an impatient restlessness, starting every time she heard a sound that might be a plane.

Minutes later, Maude came out to join her, her thin arms folded, her eyes pale and troubled. "I wish we knew something," she murmured. "Just whether or not they think he could be alive."

"He's alive," Kathryn said confidently.

Maude studied the brave little face, and a dawning light came into her eyes. "I've been very dense, haven't I, Kathryn?" she asked gently, studying the younger woman's face.

Kathryn watched the ground, reddening. "I..."

Maude put an arm around her shoulders comfortingly. "Come in and have another cup of coffee. It won't make that much difference."

"They found him!" Phillip yelled from the doorway of the terminal, his face bright, his voice full of sunlight. "The rescue plane's on its way in now!"

"Oh, thank God," Maude murmured prayerfully.

Kathryn let the tears run silently down her face unashamedly. Blake was safe. He was alive. Even if she had to give him up to Vivian, if she never saw him again, it was enough to know he'd be on the same planet with her, alive. Alive, praise God, alive!

Maude stayed outside with her, while Phillip went back inside with the others after they'd all been told the news. Kathryn couldn't be budged, and Maude stood quietly with her, waiting. Minutes passed quietly until there came the drone of a twin-engine plane. It circled the landing strip and dropped down gently, its wheels making a squealing sound briefly, lifting, then settling onto the runway.

Kathryn watched the plane with tears shimmering in her eyes, until it stopped, the engine cut off, the door opened.

A big, dark man in an open-necked shirt stepped out of it, and Kathryn was running toward him before his feet ever touched the ground.

"Blake!" she screamed, oblivious to the other members of the family coming out of the terminal behind her. She ran like a frightened child seeking refuge, her face tormented, her legs flying against the skirt of her white sundress.

He opened his arms and caught her up against him, holding her while she ground her cheek against his broad chest and wept like a wind-tossed orphan.

"Oh, Blake," she whimpered, "they said you'd gone down, and we didn't know...oh, I'd have died with you! Blake, Blake...I'd have died with you, Blake," she whispered, over and over, her voice muffled, almost incoherent, her nails stabbing into his back as she clung to him.

His big arms tightened around her, his cheek scrubbing roughly against her forehead. "I'm all right," he said. "I'm fine, Kate."

She drew away a breath and looked up at him with tears streaming down her pale face, lines of weariness and worry making her look suddenly older.

He looked older, too, his face heavily lined, his dark eyes bloodshot as if he hadn't slept in a long time. She searched his beloved face, everything she felt for him showing plainly in her green eyes.

"I love you so," she whispered brokenly. "Oh, Blake, I love you so!"

He stood there frozen, staring down at her with eyes so dark they seemed black.

Embarrassed at having been so stupidly blunt, she tugged weakly at his arms and stepped back. "I...I'm sorry," she choked. "I...didn't mean to...to throw myself at you a second time. Vivian told me...how disgusted you were yesterday," she added in a whipped tone.

"Vivian told you what?" he asked in a strange, husky whisper.

She stepped away from him, but she still clung helplessly to his big, warm hand, walking quietly beside him, the top of her head just coming to his chin, as they moved to join the others.

"It doesn't matter," she said with a painful smile. "It's all right."

"That's what you think!" he said in a voice she didn't recognize.

Vivian came running to meet him, shooting a poisonous glance at Kathryn. "Oh, Blake, darling! We were so worried!" she exclaimed, reaching up to kiss him full on the mouth. "How lovely that you're safe!"

Maude and Phillip echoed the greeting, Maude with tears misting her eyes.

"Close call?" Phillip asked with keen perception.

Blake nodded. "Too close. I wouldn't care to repeat it."

"What about the plane?" Maude asked gently.

"I'm glad it was insured," Blake replied with a faint smile. "I came down in the rain forest on Puerto Rico. The plane made it, barely, but I clipped off the wings."

Kathryn closed her eyes, seeing it in her mind.

"I'll buy you a drink," Phillip said. "You look like you could use one."

"A drink, a hot bath, and a bed," Blake agreed. He glanced at Kathryn as she moved away toward Phillip. She wouldn't meet his eyes.

"I . . . I'm going to pack," she murmured, turning away.

"Pack?" Blake asked gruffly. "Why?"

"I'm going home," she said proudly, letting her eyes meet his, only to glance off again. "I...I've had enough sun and sand. I don't like paradise...it's got too many serpents."

She turned toward the car. "Phillip, will you please drive me back to the house?" she asked with downcast eyes.

"Let Maude," he said, surprising her. "Would you mind, darling?" he asked his mother.

"No, not at all," Maude said, taking the younger girl's arm. "Come along, sweetheart. Vivian, Dick, are you coming?"

They declined, preferring to go with the men into the bar. Maude drove Kathryn home in a smothering silence.

"Don't go," Maude pleaded as Kathryn went upstairs to get her things together. "Not yet. Not today."

She turned at the head of the stairs with eyes so full of heartache they seemed to glow with it. "I can't stay here anymore," she replied softly. "I can't bear it. I...I want to look for an apartment before he..." She turned and went on upstairs. The tears choked her voice out.

She had packed everything in her bags and had changed into a neat pin-striped blue blouse and white skirt for traveling when the door opened suddenly and Blake walked in.

She stared wide-eyed at him across the bed. He looked more relaxed, but he still needed a shave and sleep.

"I...I'm almost ready," she murmured, brushing back a wild swath of long, waving dark hair from her flushed cheek. "If Phillip could drive me..."

He leaned back against the closed door and watched her. He was wearing a white shirt open halfway down the front, with dark blue trousers. His thick hair was ruffled, his face hard, his eyes narrow and dark and searching.

"The Leedses are leaving," he said quietly.

"Oh, are they?" she murmured, staring down at the white coverlet. "For how long?"

"For good. I went to Haiti to sign a contract. I'm switching the London mill to Port au Prince," he replied.

She stared at him. "But, Vivian . . ."

"Kathryn, I brought her over because I knew she was the power behind her father," he said wearily. "I knew if I could convince her to meet my terms, she'd convince him. But you misread the situation completely, and I suppose it was partially my fault. I wanted you to misread it."

She glanced at him and away. "It doesn't matter now."

"Doesn't it?" he asked softly.

"I'm going to look for an apartment when I get home, Blake," she told him, lifting her flushed young face proudly. "I want to be by myself."

He searched her eyes. "You told me you loved me, Kathryn," he said quietly, watching the color flush into her cheeks at the impact of the words.

She swallowed nervously, and traced an idle pattern on the coverlet with her finger. "I...was upset," she faltered.

"Don't play games. Don't hedge. You said you loved me. How? As a big brother—a guardian—or as a lover, Kate?"

"You're confusing me!" she protested feverishly.

"You've confused me for a solid year," he said flatly. His eyes smoldered with reined emotion. "All I do lately is slam my head against a wall trying to get through to you."

She gaped at him. "I don't understand."

He jammed his hands in his pockets and leaned back against the door, letting his eyes trace the line of her body with an intimate thoroughness.

"You never have," he replied roughly.

Her soft eyes touched the worn, weary lines in his face. "Blake, you look so tired," she said gently. "Why don't you go to bed for a while?"

"Only with you, Kate," he said shortly, watching the color go back and forth in her cheeks. "Because I'm not going to close my eyes only to open them again and find you gone.

"Donavan," he growled. "And then Phillip. My own brother, and I hated him because he could get close to you and I couldn't. And you thought that I just *wanted* you!"

Her face opened like a bud in blossom, and she stiffened, barely breathing as she listened to his deep, harsh voice.

"Wanted you!" he repeated, eyes blazing, jaw tightening. "My God, I've been out of my mind wondering whom I substituted for that night on the beach, and all along...!" He drew a short breath. "How long had you planned to keep it from me, Kathryn?" he demanded. "Were you going to go home and lock it away inside you?"

Tears were misting her eyes. She moved to the foot of the bed and held onto the bedpost, smoothing over the silky mahogany. "Blake?" she whispered.

"You told Phillip that I had to be alive, because your heart was still beating," he said in a strange, husky voice. "It was that way with me over a year ago. As long as I'm still breathing, I know you are, because there is no way on earth I could stay alive without you!"

She ran to him blindly, seeing only a big, husky blur as she reached up to be folded against him in an embrace that all but crushed the breath from her slender body.

"Kiss me," he whispered shakily, bending to take her soft mouth under his. "Kathy, Kathy, I love you so...!" he ground out against her soft, eager lips.

They kissed wildly, hungrily, and she could feel the rhythm of steel drums in her bloodstream as the pressure of his mouth became deep and intimate, expertly demanding a response she gave without restraint.

He tore his mouth away finally and buried it against her soft throat. With a sense of wonder, she felt the big arms that were holding her tremble.

"I thought you hated me," she whispered, drowning in the unbelievable sensation of loving and being loved.

"For what?" he asked gruffly. "Trying to seduce me on the beach?"

"I wasn't," she protested weakly.

"It felt like it. You'll never know exactly how close to it you came."

"I loved you so," she whispered, "and I thought I'd lost you, and I wanted one perfect memory..."

"It was that," he said softly. His arms contracted lovingly. "I'll always see you the way you looked in the moonlight, with your skin like satin, glowing..."

"Blake!" she whispered, reddening.

"Don't be embarrassed," he said quietly. "Or ashamed. It was beautiful, Kate, every second of it was beautiful. It's going to be like that every time I touch you, for the rest of our lives."

She drew away and looked up at him. "That long?" she asked.

He searched her soft green eyes. "That long. Will you marry me?"

"Yes."

He reached down and brushed her mouth with his, very gently—a seal on the promise. "I hope you like children," he murmured against her soft lips.

She smiled lazily. "How many do you want?"

"Let's get married next week and talk about it."

"Next week!" Her mouth flew open. "Blake, I can't! The invitations, and I'll have to have a gown . . . !"

He stopped the flow of words with his mouth. Through a fog of sensation, she felt his hands moving slowly, expertly, on her soft body and she moaned.

He drew back a breath. "Next week," he whispered unsteadily.

"Next week," she agreed under her breath and reached up to draw his head back down.

Outside, the sunset was lending a rose glow to the bay, where fishing boats rocked gently at the shore. And in the orange and gold swirls of color on the horizon there was a promise of blue skies ahead.

* * * * *

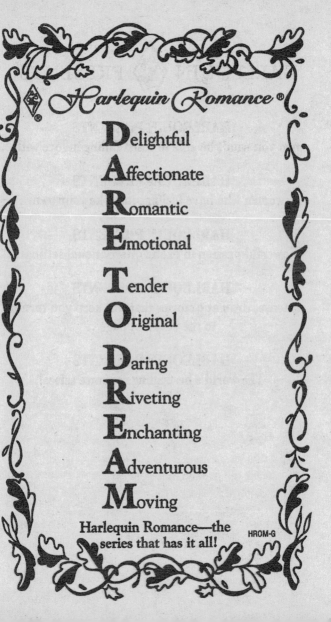

Harlequin Romance®

Delightful

Affectionate

Romantic

Emotional

Tender

Original

Daring

Riveting

Enchanting

Adventurous

Moving

Harlequin Romance—the
series that has it all!

HROM-G

HARLEQUIN PRESENTS

HARLEQUIN PRESENTS
men you won't be able to resist falling in love with...

HARLEQUIN PRESENTS
women who have feelings just like your own...

HARLEQUIN PRESENTS
powerful passion in exotic international settings...

HARLEQUIN PRESENTS
intense, dramatic stories that will keep you turning
to the very last page...

HARLEQUIN PRESENTS
The world's bestselling romance series!

Harlequin® Historical

If you're a serious fan of historical romance,
then you're in luck!

Harlequin Historicals brings you
stories by bestselling authors, rising new stars
and talented first-timers.

Ruth Langan & Theresa Michaels
Mary McBride & Cheryl St. John
Margaret Moore & Merline Lovelace
Julie Tetel & Nina Beaumont
Susan Amarillas & Ana Seymour
Deborah Simmons & Linda Castle
Cassandra Austin & Emily French
Miranda Jarrett & Suzanne Barclay
DeLoras Scott & Laurie Grant...

You'll never run out of favorites.

Harlequin Historicals...they're too good to miss!

WAYS TO *UNEXPECTEDLY* MEET MR. RIGHT:

♡ *Go out with the sexy-sounding stranger your daughter secretly set you up with through a personal ad.*

♡ *RSVP yes to a wedding invitation—soon it might be your turn to say "I do!"*

♡ *Receive a marriage proposal by mail— from a man you've never met....*

These are just a few of the unexpected ways that written communication leads to love in Silhouette Yours Truly.

Each month, look for two fast-paced, fun and flirtatious Yours Truly novels (with entertaining treats and sneak previews in the back pages) by some of your favorite authors—and some who are sure to become favorites.

YOURS TRULY™:
Love—when you least expect it!

▼ *Silhouette* ROMANCE™

What's a single dad to do when he needs a wife by next Thursday?

Who's a confirmed bachelor to call when he finds a baby on his doorstep?

How does a plain Jane in love with her gorgeous boss get him to notice her?

From classic love stories to romantic comedies to emotional heart tuggers, **Silhouette Romance** offers six irresistible novels every month by some of your favorite authors!
Such as...beloved bestsellers **Diana Palmer,**
Annette Broadrick, Suzanne Carey, Elizabeth August
and **Marie Ferrarella**, to name just a few—and some sure to become favorites!

Fabulous Fathers...Bundles of Joy...Miniseries...
Months of blushing brides and convenient weddings...
Holiday celebrations... You'll find all this and much more in
Silhouette Romance—always emotional, always enjoyable,
always about love!

John Lennon
and
Yoko Ono

On March 14, 1969, as they were being driven out of London, John and Yoko decided to get married. He asked his driver, Les Anthony, if it was possible to get married on the Channel ferry because the car was headed in that direction. They stopped at John's aunt Mimi's house to call about getting married immediately.

They could not get reservations on the ship that was departing in two hours, so John wanted to go on to Paris. Lack of passports stopped them at the Southampton ferry. John then called his office and told Peter Brown that he wanted to marry within the next half hour! Peter advised that the only place that offered instant matrimony was Gibraltar.

After spending four days secretly in Paris, they went to Gibraltar, where they had a three-minute ceremony. They returned to Paris and traveled on to the Amsterdam Hilton Hotel, where they held the first of the famous bed-ins for world peace.

B-YOKO